SHE FELL FOR A COMPTON

Savage

A NOVEL BY

ROBIN

PROLOGUE

You will be mine...

Four years earlier...

$\mathcal{T}$he cold air that was blowing through Doll's freshly straightened auburn hair gave her chills as she stood in front of her building, waiting for her usual customer to buy an eighth of weed from her. She blew air from her mouth into her hands, hoping she would warm up, but it wasn't working.

"Damn, this nigga needs to hurry up," Doll said as she looked out to the main street to see if she saw him coming.

Doll had been selling weed to everyone in her neighborhood for the last year. That was how she paid her bills, rent, and books since her mother and father stopped supporting her financially. They loved her dearly, and her and her mom were like best friends, but they felt like at the age of twenty-four, she could find a job and support herself like they had to do when they were her age and in college. However, with all the classes she was taking at King Drew University, she didn't have time for a dead-end job. She needed to use all her time to study. She got herself a medical marijuana license so she could purchase weed and started slanging on the block like she was about that life. She had one more year in school, and she knew once she got her degree, she would get a job immediately and wouldn't have to look back on the struggle life that she lived in Compton while going to school.

Doll lived on the East side of Compton in a well-kept apartment complex that was right next door to her school. The school she went to was a top medical school; however, it was located right in between Compton and Watts. Doll did not care where her school was located; once she got a scholarship to attend, she wasted no time packing her things, moving out of her parents' home in Burbank, and renting an apartment right next door to her school. It saved her money because she could walk to school instead of driving her car.

At that moment, her customer pulled up and parked in the parking lot where Doll was standing. She walked over to his car and hopped in the passenger seat. She was thankful that he had his heater blasting in his Range Rover.

"Damn, it's so fucking cold out there. I was only standing there three minutes, and I felt like I was going to freeze to death," Doll said as she placed her hands in front of the heater.

"Yeah, it's cold as fuck. But what's up with you? How is school?" Jordin asked as he reached into his pocket for his wad of cash to pay for his weed.

"School is good. I got to go in the house once I'm done out here so I can finish reading these chapters. I only have one more year left, so I have no time to slack." She passed him his weed in a white pill container.

"That's what's up. A nigga's proud of you. I've been watching you do ya school shit since you moved in my hood. That's a good look. But are you burning one with me tonight? I haven't seen you in a couple days. Thought we would catch up," Jordin said with a smirk.

Not only was she his dealer, but he was her little boy toy. It had been almost a year that he had been buying weed from her faithfully. She knew he only bought from her consistently because she liked to make out with him and let him play with her pussy in his passenger seat. Doll didn't have a man, and she had sexual needs, so she felt like Jordin was the one to fulfill them the way she liked. Jordin always told her that he thought it was a little childish that they only kissed and touched even though he was a year younger than her. She always left him with blue balls. But she knew he liked it and knew he wouldn't turn it down.

"Yeah, I can sit out here with you for a minute. Roll up," Doll said as she slid off her jacket because his heater had warmed her up.

As the two were passing the blunt back and forth and listening to music, Jordin decided to spark a conversation. He was feeling Doll and had never met a girl living in Compton that was like her. She was in school, had no kids, lived on her own, and knew how to hustle to make ends meet. However, he thought she was too beautiful and intelligent to be selling weed. He knew her struggle and her situation with school and her parents. He so badly wanted to step in and be a provider for her. That was why he always came around and bought weed from her. He didn't even have to buy from her, because he owned his own medical marijuana spot with his best friend, so he was basically giving her money because he knew she needed it. Over the last year, he had gotten to know her well enough to know that he wanted to make her his girl before some loser or schoolboy did. Jordin had a lot on his plate, but he wasn't going to let it stop him from snagging the female he wanted in his life for an eternity.

"You're going to be a nigga's wife someday. You know that?" Jordin asked out the blue as he blew smoke from his nose.

"That weed must be real good. Got you talking about marriage. Let me hit it again so I can feel the same way," Doll joked.

"Nah, I'm for real. I've been buying weed from you that I don't even need. I end up giving it to my homies. I knew if I bought weed from you, I could snag some of your time every time I came through, to get to know you. And you've told me enough to want to wife you."

Doll smiled. "I'm flattered ... So you've been giving my weed away, huh? What? You don't like it or something?" Doll asked, slightly changing the subject. Him talking about marriage made her a little nervous. Getting married was something she always wanted to do, but knew it wouldn't happen anytime soon.

He chuckled. "I mean, it could be better. But I own a weed shop. I thought you would have asked about me by now to know what I be doing around here."

"No, I only go off what you tell me, which is not too much. We spend most the night talking about me until you got your tongue down my throat. It's like I've been kissing a stranger and letting him play in my pussy for a year, and that's only because you have nice conversation, and you are cute, so I think that's as far as it will ever get with us. I may not know much, but my friend tells me you got a girl, so don't even try to lead me on." She crossed her arms.

"I don't have a girl. That's why I want to make you my wife. And I won't take no for an answer." Jordin gazed at her, hoping his boldness would make her say yes.

Doll looked Jordin in his eyes. She was trying to find some kind of dishonesty in his gaze so she could tell his ass no. But the look he gave her told her that he was serious. She had never made someone her man over a smoke session and a simple demand. But there was something about Jordin that she liked too. She hadn't had a boyfriend since high school, because she felt like her life was too busy for a boyfriend. But something about this man that was staring at her like he could see their future right before his eyes made her think that, just maybe, she could fit him into her life. Maybe life would be easier if she opened her heart to this stranger that cared so much to waste money on weed he didn't need just to get to know her and steal a little of her time. However, she still needed answers of her own before she gave him any kind of answer.

"What do you want from me, Jordin? I'm sure women drool over you every day around here. And how do I know for sure you don't have a girl?"

"Trust me, ain't no bitch in my life worthy enough for me to make them my girl. I mean, I got bitches around me, but they just be homegirls and bitches that budtend at my shop. But I'm single, and all I want from you is your heart and your trust. Let me take some of that weight off ya back so you don't have to be out here slanging weed. It's dangerous, so let me come in your life and be that nigga you need. I promise I won't disappoint you." He took his index finger and lifted her chin to make sure she made eye contact with him.

Their gaze turned into their usual make out session. But this time, their kiss was passionate and real. It wasn't like the high-school make-out sessions they usually had. This kiss had emotion and had Doll feeling like she could someday fall in love.

Doll disconnected their kiss, and Jordin was in a daze. He had never had a woman make him feel so good and so connected. Her lips had him in a bewilderment that he didn't want to come out of, even though Doll still hadn't given him his answer.

"Jordin, I believe in real love and marriage. Are you ready for that commitment? Are you ready to build something real with me?"

"Dollaysia, I'd marry you tonight if City Hall was open; that's how much I like you. I think about you every day, and I'm finally comfortable to ask you. Now are you going to be my girl or not?" Jordin was anxious to know her answer.

Doll slid her shoes off and climbed over to the passenger side and straddled herself in his lap. "I'll be your girl, Jordin. But no sex until our six-month anniversary. I want to get to know you more before I give you my all. And if you want to marry me like you say, you will wait for your future wifey."

"I'll wait forever, lil' mama. Whatever you want," Jordin said. He was to the point to where he would do anything for Doll. She was the one, and there was no denying it anymore. He had stayed up late nights, trying to find all the right reasons why he wanted to be with Doll, and now he knew. Therefore, whatever it took to get her to carry his last name, he was going to do it.

"Well, I guess I'm yours then." She smiled as she stroked his face with her the palm of her hand. She saw how beautiful his brown eyes were and how flawless his chocolate, brown skin was. His teeth weren't the straightest, but they were white, and his breath was always fresh. She had a man, and it was unexpected. But her mother always told her that the man that was unexpected was more than likely the man for you.

Jordin pulled her face closer, and they shared a passionate kiss again. He was so happy she had said yes. He was so tired of dealing with the females around him, so he felt like having someone solid like Doll in his life would change him and make him a better man even though he was so young. He was going to try his hardest to not let his street life get in the way of his relationship.

"I have to go in the house now, though. Since I'm your girl, call me. We have a lot to talk about. Now it's time for you to tell me about you." She climbed off his lap.

"Bet … Soon as I get to my shop, I'll call you. I want to bring you in tomorrow if you have time, so you can see what I do to get money."

"I get out of school at three, so it's a date."

Doll got out of Jordin's truck in awe. She couldn't believe that she had made it official with him on such short notice. But Jordin had a way with words that had her mind gone. She was confident he wouldn't let her down, but just in case, she was sticking to her six-month rule.

Doll passed up her house and walked to the other side of the building to her best friend Breann's house. Breann and Doll had been friends ever since Doll moved in the building. While everyone that hung out in the building gave her the cold shoulder because she wasn't from around there, Breann welcomed her with open arms, and they had been friends ever since.

Doll knocked on her gate frequently as her finger rang her bell outside of her gate. Each apartment had a gate that led to everyone's personal patio and front door. Breann opened her door quickly.

"Open the gate, bitch! I got some news for you," Doll said with a huge smile on her face.

"Bitch, don't be ringing my bell like that, like you the police. And it better be some good damn news because my man will be here in a minute, and I don't want nobody here," Breann said as she opened her gate.

"Okay, I won't be long, because I have to go study."

The girls walked into Breann's house, out of the cold, and she closed the door. They walked into her decked-out living room that she had dressed in leopard and black. Her couches were black with leopard pillows and a throw cover. She had a leopard table rug under her coffee table with black blinds she had custom put in her apartment.

"You won't believe what the fuck I just did," Doll said as she continued to smile.

"What, bitch? Finally find you a nigga and got some dick?" Breann asked as she picked up her blunt and lighter from the table.

"Close … I made it official with Jordin." She smiled again. However,

Breann wasn't smiling.

"You did what?" she asked again as if her ears were deceiving her.

"You heard me. He asked me, and I said yes. But we won't be having sex for six months …"

"Yeah, you won't be having sex for six months, but he certainly will. I told you the nigga got a girl. And if the bitch ain't his girl, she surely is his hoe, the way she be with him. I'm not trying to cramp your style, and I knew you been had a little thing for him, but you don't know these niggas around here like I do. They prey on good girls like you. Next thing you know, the nigga will be moving you out the hood and away from his other bitches. But if this is what you want, by all means, I'm for it." Breann shrugged and puffed her blunt.

"Well, since you know so much, does he really own a weed shop?" Doll asked with a slight attitude.

"Yeah, he does. He owns it with my man. They are best friends; that's why I know so much about Jordin. He's a scum, but maybe your cute ass can change him. You know I got your back if you need me. I'll fuck a bitch up over you," she said in a serious tone.

Doll laughed. "I know you will have my back, bitch, so what is this girl's name? Tell me more about her," Doll said in a curious tone.

"Her name is Tiffany. She works at his shop, but they are always together. I've known this bitch since middle school, and I know she is a hoe. He might be telling you the truth about not having a girlfriend. She might just be sucking his dick, and she's finally getting replaced by you."

"Well, I'm going to keep an eye out on this bitch when I see who she is. And if he lied to me, it's over before it even starts." She crossed her arms.

"Well, you were smart, hitting him with the six-month rule. I hate to kick you out, though, but my man is about to come. Go cake up with yours on the phone because I know that's what y'all about to do." She stood up from the couch.

"We sure are. I'll come over after school."

The girls hugged, and Breann let Doll out. Doll went straight home and called Jordin while she went over her notes ...

$$\$\$\$\$\$\$$$

Two days later...

Doll adjusted her heavy backpack as she walked out of her school to head home. Her head was pounding, and all she wanted to do was climb in bed and sleep. It was Thursday, so she knew she would be sleeping in the following day. She was so tired that she could envision herself already enjoying her usual three-day weekend. As she walked through the parking lot that led to 120th Street where her apartment was, she heard someone call her name. She looked around and spotted Jordin leaning on the hood of his truck.

"Aye, Doll. Check it out," Jordin said.

Doll walked over to Jordin. She figured he could make her life easier at that moment and drive her home.

"What's up, Jordin? What are you doing here?"

"What's up, cutie? I'm sorry I couldn't make it yesterday, so I thought I'd come pick my lady up from school and have her ride with me for the rest of the day. I was thinking stop by my shop to meet my crew and then go to dinner," Jordin said with a smile.

"Oh …" Doll said in a bitter tone. The only place she wanted to go was home.

"Oh? What's wrong? You must've forgotten we made it official two nights ago, and I said I wanted to show you what I do for a living." He laughed a little. He was feeling a little embarrassed that she wasn't happy to see him, but he kept his cool.

"Kind of …"

Jordin's eyes widened. "Wow, well … let me refresh your memory." He lifted her chin and kissed her lips softly, taking in her bottom lip the way she liked.

Doll tightened her legs when she felt her clit tingle from his kiss. That indeed reminded her that they were now a couple. She loved the way Jordin kissed her. It always sent her into a daze.

"So are you riding with me, babe? I want you to meet my staff and my friends. Aren't you trying to get to know me?"

Doll couldn't say no to those beautiful brown eyes and sincere face he was wearing. She thought it was nice that he was already ready to introduce her to his friends.

"Yeah, I'll go with you. But I'm tired, so I don't want to be out too long."

"I promise we won't be there no longer than two hours."

He opened the car door and slid her backpack off her back. "No wonder your school-girl ass be tired. This shit is heavy!" Jordin expressed as he tossed her backpack in the backseat.

She laughed as she rested her head on the seat. "Yup, I'm a real school girl."

Ten minutes later, Jordin pulled into the back of his shop that was located on Compton Avenue and parked. He got out and opened the door for Doll. They then walked to the steel door, and Jordin opened it with a bronze-colored key. As they walked down the hall to the front of the shop, he gripped her hand and intertwined their fingers together. He then kissed the top of her hand. He was ready to let everyone know that she was his girl, and he was proud. However, Doll was nervous and didn't know how his friends would look at her. She was cute, but she always considered herself as average. And the way Jordin shined, she knew people were going to wonder what he was doing with her.

Before they walked to the front fully, Doll stopped them from walking. "Wait, Jordin … You don't think it's too early to meet your friends? It's only been two days, and I haven't talked to you since the night we got together. I mean, what if they look at me weird? My hair is a mess, and I have on bleached jeans. What am I supposed to say?" she asked nervously above a whisper.

Jordin chuckled as he watched her brown skin almost turn burgundy. "Don't worry about how they see you; all you need to know is that you are beautiful to me. They are going to respect whoever I choose to be in a relationship with, so I'm going to introduce you, and then you can just wave if that's all you want to do."

Doll sighed as she looked at him with her puppy dog eyes that Jordin always got lost in. "Okay. Well, let's do this."

They then walked into the front of the shop. Music was blasting while his workers served people at the counter some of the best weed you could buy. The shop was damn near packed, so Doll knew he had to be bringing in a lot of money. She looked behind the counter and saw he only had female workers. There were men standing behind them, watching how much weed they weighed out to customers and making sure the customers didn't try to pull any funny business on the women.

"My nigga, Mercy, you finally made it to work. What you doin' with School Girl?" Jordin's best friend asked with a huge smile on his face.

"Oh, you know her? She's my lady now. You ain't gotta call her School Girl, though. Her name is Doll."

"Oh, my bad, bro. It's nice seeing you again. She's Breann's lil' best friend. I told Bre you are the only friend she has with some sense. You're lucky, my nigga. She's a good girl," he laughed.

"Yeah, Bre is my girl. I don't know what I'd do without her," she smiled.

"Yeah, she says the same shit. Nigga, we done made about 60k today, so I'm going to clear these drawers and count this cash in the stash room. Check me out before y'all leave."

The two gave each other daps, and Jordin and Doll walked behind the counter. Jordin then started introducing her to everyone, and they welcomed her with open arms.

"She's cute, Mercy. You better treat her right because you know don't nobody want your hood ass, so you're lucky," his budtender, Alaina, said as she laughed.

"Shut up, Alaina. I am going to treat her right. That's why I brought her here to meet the crew. She is going to be around a lot, and I want y'all to treat her with the same respect y'all show me," Jordin said with a serious look on his face.

"I ain't gotta show nobody respect," his head budtender, Tiffany, said as she walked up to Jordin, Alaina, and Doll.

Doll looked at the woman and frowned a little bit.

Jordin frowned as well. He hated when Tiffany thought she could say what she wanted. "Don't start that bullshit, Tiffany. This my girl now, so if I say you gotta respect her, that's what you gonna do."

"Whatever, Mercy. What's your name?" Tiffany asked as she popped on her gum. Doll was already not feeling her and knew she would be a problem. But she kept her cool.

"My name is Doll ..."

"Mmm. Well, it's nice meeting you. Mercy never brings his bitches around us, so that says a lot about you. I'm about to get to work. It's money to be made. Not all of us around here can snatch a baller," Tiffany said as she walked off to serve a customer.

"She's just a hater. Don't mind her," Alaina said as she shook her head.

"I'm the least worried," Doll said as she eyed Tiffany. She knew that was the girl that Breann had warned her about. She knew she couldn't possibly be Jordin's girlfriend. She knew if that was his girl, she would have raised hell that he had walked in with another woman and openly let everyone know that they were together.

Doll brushed off her thoughts as Jordin walked her to the back. They then headed down the hall to his office. He unlocked the door, and they walked in. The cold air from the AC brushed across their faces as they made their way to his desk. His office was nice and cozy. He had a couch and a huge oak wood desk. He had a TV hanging on the wall with a bud bar and liquor bar in the corner. Jordin turned on the TV, and they both sat at his desk.

"So who is Mercy?" Doll asked, interested in why everyone was calling him that name.

"That's me. That's my hood name." He smirked and sat behind his desk.

"Your hood name, huh? So you are in the streets like that? I hope you won't be putting me in harm's way." She raised her eyebrow.

"I'll never put you in harm's way, and that's a fact. And if any of them niggas over there in them apartments try you in anyway when they see you are my girl, you let me know. I got somethin' for they asses." Jordin pulled his 9mm from his waist and sat it on the table.

Doll eyed it, and then she looked up at him. "You're crazy. Don't have me thinking this is a mistake. And what's up with your budtender, Tiffany? I heard she's the one that's supposed to be your girl." She crossed her arms and looked at him with a slight attitude.

"That bitch ain't my girl. She just works here. You ain't gotta worry about her either, tho'. She can get it too. So how much do you pay for school every month?" Jordin asked as he reached into his desk drawer while gradually changing the subject.

"I better not have to worry about her … And I don't pay anything for school. I'm on a scholarship. I pay for books when I need to, and that's three hundred a book. I pay my rent, which is nine hundred a month, and all my bills, so I'm dishing out $1,300 every month on living, and that's not even counting food, clothes, my nails, and my hair ..."

Jordin pulled a stack of money from his desk drawer. He then pulled the money machine that was sitting on his desk closer to him and slid the stack of money through it after he turned it on. He counted out 5K from the 10K he had.

"Here's five-grand. That should take care the things you need to take care of for right now. If you need more, let me now." He slid the money across the table, but Doll slid it back.

"I'm not a charity case, Jordin. You don't have to take care of me. I'll be graduating school in a year, and I'll be able to work at the hospital full time. I get money selling my weed, and I'm content with what I do. I don't want to depend on you."

"You are my girl, and I don't have no plans on us ever not being together. I'm not going to have you out here selling bunk ass weed. I wanna do what a nigga's supposed to do for his girl, especially since I got it. I don't look at you as a charity case. I look at you as my woman. Now take the money, babe." He slid it back to her.

She eyed the money before she picked it up. She knew she needed the money, and her weed sales were slowly slowing down since people were going to Jordin's shop to buy weed. She was tired of selling it anyway because people always wanted a discount. Therefore, she took the money.

"Thank you, Jordin. This means a lot."

"I'm glad it does. Don't ever hesitate to ask me for shit. I got you … I promise."

Jordin stood up and walked over to Doll. He grabbed her hand and made her stand up. He took her in for a hug. That was the first time she had hugged Jordin and felt safe. The way he talked to her always sounded so sincere, and she was hoping she wasn't making a mistake with moving so fast with him. She did want to be in a relationship and wanted to soon get married.

She always remembered her parents' love story and how they met. They had been together thirty years and met while Christmas shopping. She remembered her father telling her how much he was in love with her mother when he saw her walking through Macy's department store with her mother. After they exchanged numbers, they hit it off that same week and got married six months later and had been together ever since. That was the kind of love that Doll wanted, and she was hoping Jordin was ready for that.

"I hope you don't break my heart, Jordin."

"I promise I won't. I'm going to go back to the front, tho'. You can come up there if you want, or you can stay back here and chill."

Doll looked around the office. It looked so cozy, and the cold air was making her sleepy.

"No, I'd rather go home or stay back here."

"I'll take you home later. Just stay back here and get some rest. Ain't nobody going to fuck with you."

After Jordin left out of his office, he locked the door, making sure nobody could come in and disturb her. She then laid back on the comfortable couch and threw the cover over her that was thrown over the couch. Before she knew it, she was in a deep sleep.

$$$$$

"Dollaysia, wake up. I'm about to take you to get something to eat, and then I'm going to take you home," Doll heard Jordin's voice as she opened her eyes.

She sat up and stretched her arms. "Damn, what time is it? I was sleeping good," Doll said in a sleepy tone.

"Yeah, I can tell with the drool stains on your face," he chuckled. "But it's almost eleven."

"Almost eleven? It was three thirty when I got here. We can go through a drive-thru. I'm just ready to go home." She stood up and picked up her purse. She pulled out her compact mirror, and she looked a mess. Her hair was frizzy, she had drool on her face, and she had black circles around her eyes. She hated when she got black circles, and she was a little embarrassed of her appearance.

"I'm sorry about that, but I left and ran some errands. When came back, I checked in on you, but you were out, so I went up front and served a few people."

"It's okay. I actually like sleeping back here; it's quiet. Might be my new napping place when I'm here."

"You can sleep here anytime you want to."

After they left Jordin's shop, they went through Tam's Burger drive-thru and headed to her apartments. He parked in the parking lot, and they both got out his truck.

"I'm glad you agreed to meet my niggas. They really like you and think you are going to change a nigga's life," Jordin said as he grabbed her waist and pulled her close.

"And what makes them say that?"

"I've done a lot of shit in my life that ain't good. And every female I've been with has been on the same level as me. They like the streets and dirty money. I want somebody that's about business and the finer things in life. I can see that in you. I got the money to live how I want, but I wanted a real woman to share it with me. It's more where today came from, and I promise I'm going to show you some shit no nigga will ever be able to show you."

"You're just gassin', Jordin. But since you are going to show me better than you can tell me, I'll be waiting. I'm glad your friends feel that way about me, tho."

"I'm not gassing at all. I wanna marry you."

Out of nowhere, Jordin pulled out a necklace box from his hoodie pocket and opened it. It was a small rope chain with an engagement ring as the charm. He smiled.

"Oh, no, Jordin. Now you are moving way too fast—"

He cut her off before she got ahead of herself. "Let me speak. This isn't an engagement. This is a promise. A promise that in six months, if I'm worthy, you will wear this ring. I want you to wear the necklace and put the ring on when you are ready to commit to me a hundred percent."

Doll gazed at the chain and the necklace. It was nice, but she wasn't sure if she wanted to take it. It was too soon and a little overwhelming for her. She had never had a man buy her jewelry or give her money. The only man that bought her jewelry was her father, but that was different for her. She knew the only time men did these kinds of things for a woman was when he was in love. She looked at Jordin as he held the box open, waiting for her to accept it.

"Are you in love with me, Jordin? Men only do this for women they love." Doll said.

Jordin thought about her question. *Was he in love?* He hadn't thought that out; he just knew he had a soft spot for her and wanted to be in her life. Everyone around him acted as if she were lucky to be with him, when in truth, he felt like he was lucky to be let into her world. Doll was reserved and didn't like too many people around her. She had told him on so many occasions when they sat up and talked in his truck that she didn't like too many people in her space. Jordin and Breann were the first people she let get close to her since she had moved from Burbank and started school. She had classmates as friends, but she didn't hang with them. And her friends in Burbank, she left them behind, so Jordin wanted to cherish being in her world.

"Maybe I am in love. You are showing me a side of me that I never knew I had. I just want to love on you and give you the world, so if that's what being in love is, I guess I am." He shrugged. He was a little surprised at his own words.

"I'll accept your necklace then. I can't tell you if I'm in love or not yet. But just know your hood ass is growing on me. You're different than you portray to be in the streets. You are really loving and caring." She smiled and took the necklace box.

Jordin let out a sigh of relief when she took the box. When she was sleep, he and Janario went to the jewelry store and bought the necklace and ring. Even Janario thought he was moving too fast, but Jordin was following his own heart.

After Jordin walked her to her apartment and kissed her goodnight, he headed back to his truck with his heart on his sleeve. Doll had him in a great mood, but before he could even get three feet away from her house, two niggas approached him out the dark. They had black bandannas covering their faces. One of the men walked up to Jordin and put his gun to his stomach.

"What's up, you bitch ass nigga? You ready to die tonight?" the man asked as he continued to point his gun in Jordin's stomach. He was ready to blow Jordin's insides up.

"Who the fuck sent you lame ass niggas?" Jordin asked with a smirk.

"Don't worry about who sent me, nigga!"

Jordin and the two dudes began to scuffle, and the boy shot Jordin in the stomach. Jordin fell to the ground, and he felt the burning bullet tear through his intestines. The two dudes ran off, leaving Jordin to bleed to death.

Doll stood in her kitchen, gazing at her necklace, when she heard a loud gunshot coming from outside. It startled her, causing her to jump.

"*Jordin,*" she thought, quickly realizing it was a gunshot. She ran outside and saw Jordin sitting hunched over, holding his stomach. Doll ran over to him.

"Oh my God, Jordin, what happened?" Doll asked as she examined him. That was when she saw blood all over his hands as he continued to hold his stomach.

"Bitch ass niggas shot me in the stomach. Help me up and drive across the street to the hospital," Jordin said as he spat up blood.

Tears flooded her face as she helped him up. She could hardly see because the tears were coming down so much. He was moaning in pain, and they had a little stretch to his truck. She couldn't believe somebody had shot Jordin. She was so scared and hoped he didn't die.

Doll helped him into his passenger side and grabbed his keys from his hands. She started up his truck and immediately raced to MLK Hospital that was located across the street from where she lived. The area was full of gangs but surrounded by a medical school and a huge hospital that specialized in gunshot wounds.

Doll pulled into the emergency area and ran out of the truck. "Somebody help me, please! My boyfriend was shot in the stomach!" she shouted in the lobby of the emergency room. Nurses and EMT's that were there rushed out to Jordin's truck. They could see the blood all over her clothes and the blood she had smeared on her face from wiping her tears away. By the time they got outside to Jordin, he was going into shock.

"Ma'am, can you tell us what happened to him?" an officer asked Doll as the doctors rushed Jordin off to surgery.

"I don't know. I just heard gunshots from my kitchen, and I ran outside to see if he was okay. He had just left my house. I didn't see anyone," Doll said in a shaky tone. Her hands were shaking, and she couldn't stop crying.

"Okay, well just stay here. They rushed him to surgery. Does he have any family?"

"Yes, he has his mother, and his best friend. I'll call them right away. His phone is in his truck."

"Okay, contact his family. He isn't doing too good." The officer walked off.

Doll rushed to his truck, and the first person she called was Janario.

"Janario, Jordin was shot in the apartments. I think he's going to die. I'm at MLK Hospital!" Doll cried out.

"What? Aight, I'm on my way." He hung up immediately.

Doll sat in his driver's seat, praying and crying. She was hoping he pulled through because she knew that him dying would be something she would never forget.

$$\$\$\$\$\$\$$$

Doll sat next to Jordin's bed in ICU with prayer beads in her hand. Jordin was on heavy medication, and he hadn't been up in a week. She was so worried about him, and doctors thought for sure he was going to die. She felt so bad for him and had been coming to see him every day after school. It was a Thursday, so she decided to stay the weekend with him. Doll stood up and walked to his bed. She then looked under the cover that was lying across him and looked at his staples in his stomach. He had fifty staples from his pelvis to his chest. He had to shit in a colostomy bag, and he had drains coming from his stomach as well. She covered her mouth. That was her first time seeing his scar. She knew if he pulled through, it was going to be a while before he was his normal self again.

"How's he doing?" Doll heard a voice ask from behind her.

When she turned around, it was a short, dark-skinned woman. She was wearing a mini skirt and a dingy, white, fur jacket. The heels on her feet showed they had done a lot of walking and made a lot of money doing it.

"Hey, not too good … He's on the highest dose of pain meds, and they are talking about putting him on a ventilator." Doll sat back down and put her beads away. She didn't know who the woman was, but she seemed concerned, so she knew she had to be a relative.

The woman sat her bag down and then walked over to the bed Jordin was lying in. She took her index finger and rubbed it down his cheek. She smiled. "I remember when I had this big head boy. He came out silent with a mean mug. Right then, I knew he was going to be something else."

"Are you his mother?" Doll asked in a soft tone as she gazed at the woman.

"Yes, I am, and I love him to death, even when he thinks I don't. Jordin is a good boy, but them streets got the best of him, and it's my fault. He's a menace, but he doesn't deserve this." His mother began to cry.

She walked around the bed and sat next to Doll. She then put her head in her lap and started crying harder. Doll rubbed her back as his mother continued to weep.

"I taught him everything about the streets. I was homeless with him for ten years. We were in and out of shelters, motels, and dope houses. If I would have just got my shit together, he would have never known about the streets!" His mother was telling her things about Jordin that she didn't know. She wondered how his childhood was and who raised him, and here his mother was, pouring her heart out to her.

"Jordin is going to be okay. He's been changing his life and saying he wants to get out the hood for good. You did all you could. He still loves you." Doll was trying to sympathize with her. Her son was on his deathbed.

His mother looked at Doll. She reminded her so much of herself when she was young. She was pretty, and her skin glowed like hers used to do. After years of doing drugs and being a prostitute, she lost her beauty and her glow. She had just spoken with Jordin a couple days before. She came to his shop to get a few dollars, and he told her about Doll and showed her a picture. She and Jordin had a good relationship and had always been tight. He was his mother's protector, and if anyone fucked with her, she could call him to clean up the mess. She knew her son was trying to do right, but she knew those streets had a hold on him so tight that he was going to need more than a woman to escape it.

"You must be the new girlfriend he was telling me about." She wiped away her tears and smiled.

Doll smiled back. "Yes, I am."

"Well, from what I hear, he's lucky to have a girl like you. These street women are nothing but trouble, so you stay in school and continue to do good, even if he doesn't make it." She stood up. "Thank you for being here for my son, tho'. That Tiffany girl was probably the reason he's laid up in this bed now." She grabbed her purse and walked out the room.

Doll sighed and then placed her eyes on Jordin. She knew he had a lot of baggage, and she was hoping it never got too overwhelming for her. She felt like she was putting her life on the line for him, so she was hoping he was worth it…

CHAPTER ONE

It's our wedding day...

Six months later...

$\mathcal{D}$oll stepped out of her car and brushed her beautiful, tight pencil dress with a lint roller. It was white and snugged her body perfectly. She then threw her long, black hair to her back and walked on the curb, ready to enter Jordin's shop. It was finally their six-month anniversary, and she couldn't have been happier. She and Jordin made it to the six-month mark, and she was ready to take him up on his offer and give him her all. After he got shot and survived, it brought them closer together. She spent every day in his hospital room, helping the nurses nurse him back to health. She wasn't a nurse, but going to school for Lab Technician taught her a lot about the human body.

She dressed up in all white, ready to accept his hand in marriage. But she wanted to surprise him about agreeing to marry him. She didn't care that they would be only going down to City Hall to tie the knot. All she knew is she wanted to wear his last name. Neither of them had time to plan a wedding anyway, so the deal was to marry and go on a honeymoon trip in Laughlin, Nevada, if she made up her mind to marry him.

When she walked into the shop, the smell of Kush brushed across her nose as Dr. Dre's Chronic blared through the shop. The coffee bean smell from the top-shelf Kush instantly made her want to take a puff, but she had other things on her mind. And that was getting to City Hall and marrying the love of her life before it closed.

As she walked past the counter, everyone that worked there and everyone buying weed scoped out her appearance. She looked flawless in her mini-skirt, and everyone wondered what the occasion was. Doll walked up to the door that led to the back of the shop so she could get in. She hit the buzzer, and one of his budtenders, Tiffany, walked to the door.

"May I help you?" Tiffany asked in a sassy tone as she chewed on her gum.

"Yes, you know I'm here for Jordin, so can you let me back?" Doll asked.

She and Tiffany didn't particularly like each other since the day Jordin introduced them. Tiffany was the face of the store, and she had brought in most of Jordin's top customers. But Doll didn't care about her position as one of Jordin's employees. Jordin was her man, and being his girl was a higher position than Tiffany would ever have.

Tiffany was only five four in height with the body of a toothpick, but her attitude and gangsta ways made her appear big. She was from Compton as well and from the same hood as Jordin. Now, she even lived in the same building as Breann and Doll, so the tension was higher than it was before. Jordin brought her in because she was a good look and brought money in, but Doll always told him he could hire someone else that was as twice as good looking as her and had a better attitude.

Tiffany wasn't ugly, but you could tell from the faint scars on her face that she had been through a lot and still going through it. She wore her hair shaved on the left side with midnight Blue weave covering the rest of her head. Doll always wore her hair dark orange or jet black. She always thought the blue was ghetto. But seeing Tiffany was from Compton, Doll assumed, *It's a Compton Thing.*

"Let me call back there and see if he's here." Tiffany pulled out her phone.

Doll smirked. "He's here. I saw his Porsche truck, and I already talked to him. Now let me in." Doll put her hand on her hip.

She was becoming agitated with the stalling Tiffany was doing. She had less than two hours to marry Jordin on their anniversary, and Tiffany was being a bitch. In the pit of her gut, she felt that Tiffany had a thing for Jordin. She was always in his office, and she was so overprotective of him when Doll came around. Every time she saw Doll, she acted as if she did not know who she was or what her position was in Jordin's life.

Tiffany rolled her eyes and buzzed the door open to let Doll in. Tiffany stepped to the side and watched Doll walk off.

Why the fuck is this bitch so dressed up in all white? Tiffany wondered as she turned up her nose at Doll's Giuseppe heels. *That nigga Jordin really upgraded this bitch,* Tiffany said to herself again.

When she first met Doll, she was wearing cheap Target jeans and a Hollister sweater. Now, she was wearing three-thousand-dollar heels. *I wish I had a nigga to upgrade me,* was her last thought as she walked back to the counter and tended to a customer.

Doll made her way to the back. Jordin's office was out of eye's reach from the front and located at the very back of the building near the back exit. As she got to know Jordin, she noticed he didn't like to be seen much and would rather remain low key and count his money behind the scenes. She liked that about him because everyone didn't know who they were on the outside world. She didn't like attention too much either, so living the reserved life with him was good for her.

Doll knocked on the door twice like Jordin always requested of everyone. Within seconds, the door unlocked, and a huge guy dressed in black opened the door. It was Jordin's security, Brian, for the store.

"What's up, sis? How are you today?" Brian asked with a smile. He looked mean and rugged, but he was a sweetheart every time he saw Doll.

"I'm doing great, big guy. It's my anniversary." She walked into the office.

"I heard ..."

Jordin looked up from the piece of paper he was reading and saw Doll looking her best. He smiled at her appearance. She was blossoming into a classy woman right before him. She was a jeans kind of girl, but after Jordin told her he liked when she dressed up in her best, she started doing it more often. But today, she looked like a million bucks. Jordin picked up the two dozen white roses he got for her from his desk and stood up with his crutch to greet her. It had been six months since he had gotten shot, and the doctor insisted he stayed on crutches for another month even though he was just about healed. He thanked Doll every day for being there for him when nobody else was.

"Happy Anniversary, baby. I got these for you. I never bought anyone flowers but my mama, so this is big for me," Jordin admitted as he handed her the beautiful flowers.

Doll took the flowers and sniffed them. She smiled. "I love them. Thank you." She then took Jordin into her arms. They hugged and kissed for what seemed like an eternity.

"I'ma leave you two lovebirds alone. I'll be in the front, searching niggas that come in lookin' suspicious," his body guard said as he walked out the office.

When they let each other go, they sat on the couch that was in his office.

"So what do you want to do today. I was thinking dinner and get a room," Jordin said.

"Ehh … I was thinking get married." She smiled and put her hand on his leg. She was wearing the engagement ring that she had been wearing on her necklace he had given her six months ago.

Jordin smiled, almost blushing. He then cleared his throat so he could speak. "Damn, are you for real?" he asked, slightly nervous.

"Yeah … That's what you want, right? You want forever, right?" Doll grabbed his hands.

"Yea-yeah, that's what I want. Well, let's get out of here then. City

Hall closes in a couple hours." Jordin stood up and grabbed her hand. He was dressed in a white polo shirt and a pair of black jeans. He wasn't dressed to get married, but dressed enough to look good in a picture or two.

"Wait, we don't have a witness," Jordin said before they walked out of his office.

"I got that covered. Breann is waiting for us. Now let's go!" Doll said with a laugh as she pointed at her small gold watch.

Jordin grabbed her hand, and they walked to the front. Jordin turned the music off, and everyone looked at him and Doll as they smiled at everyone.

"What's up, boss man? Why you turn the music off?" Alaina asked.

"I just wanted to make an announcement that today is me and my lady's six-month anniversary, and we are off to get married, so I won't be in for a week. Y'all enjoy the rest of y'all day. Edibles are on the house for the next hour," Jordin said. He was feeling great and knew he could afford to give out free weed brownies as a celebration. He and Doll walked out the door and got into her car, leaving everyone cheering and celebrating for them.

Except Tiffany...

Tiffany stormed off to the bathroom and slammed the door. Alaina and Jordin's other budtender Stacy began to laugh when they saw Tiffany run off.

"She must be still checking for Mercy. That's a damn shame," Stacy said as she shook her head.

"I'm sure she is, and you know she had to make a mini scene. I'm happy he announced his wedding. Now I bet she will leave that nigga alone," Ariana responded.

"Yeah right. She is forever going to be one of Mercy's tag-a-long groupies."

The girls laughed and continued to serve customers that came in…

$$$$$

Jordin and Doll left the Compton Courthouse all smiles. After having to wait an hour, they were able to have a quick ceremony and then sign their marriage license. Doll felt like the luckiest woman in the world walking out that court building with her man and her best friend.

"I'm so happy for y'all. But I'm about to get out of here. Janario is waiting for me at home," Breann said as she hugged Doll.

"Alright, Bre. Thanks for being our witness. Tell that nigga Janario I'm going to get at him in a week," Jordin said as he hugged Breann as well. Jordin wasn't handling any business until he came back from Nevada with his new wife.

When Breann walked off to her car, Doll looked at Jordin. "So now what, hubby?" Doll asked with a smile.

"I have a surprise for you that I think you are going to like, and I hope you accept."

"What is it?"

"I'll show you when we get there."

Jordin took her on a thirty-five-minute drive to Pomona, California. It was a small city not too far from Los Angeles. Jordin drove them through a nice neighborhood with brand new homes. Doll looked at all the beautiful homes and wished one of them were hers. She always wanted a big house with a husband and a couple of kids like her parents.

"These houses are so nice. You wouldn't even believe it was Pomona, the way people talk so bad about this city," Doll said as she continued to gaze out the window.

"Yeah, I know. I like it here."

Moments later, they pulled in the driveway of a beautiful gray home. It looked as if it were two stories. The grass was freshly manicured, and the sprinklers were on.

"Whose house is this?" Doll asked as she took off her seatbelt.

"You'll see … Get out."

The two of them got out of the car and walked to the huge wooden front door. Jordin unlocked the door with one of the keys on his key ring and opened the door. When they walked in, the sensored lights came on automatically.

"Wow, this is nice," Doll said as they walked down the foyer and into the living room.

Jordin smiled. "You like it?"

"So far, yeah. But where are the people that live here?" Doll asked in a curious tone.

"We are the people that live here," he smiled.

"What?" Doll asked, almost speechless.

"This is our home, babe. I used to live here alone, but I'm hardly here. Now I will have a reason to come home if you stay here with me."

"But it's empty. You've been living in an empty home?"

Jordin laughed. "Nah … I sold all my furniture, got it renovated. Now I'm leaving the decorating to you." He reached into his wallet and pulled out a debit card. He handed it to her.

"I-I don't know, Jordin. I have school, and this is way too far."

"Don't worry about that. You have a car, and you have me. Don't worry about expenses. You don't have to worry about that anymore. Just say 'yes, you will move with me.'" He looked at her with pleading eyes.

"I guess so. You are my husband now, so if you want me to move with you, I will."

He smiled. "Well, let me show you around this big motherfucka!" Jordin said in excitement.

Doll was in awe as she walked around the huge family home. There were four bedrooms and five bathrooms. There was a den, a basement, and a pool in the backyard. As they walked into every room, Doll took notes in her mind on how she wanted to decorate each room. She even had designs for a kid's room. Finally making it to the end of the hall, they made it to the master bedroom. It was empty and full of space. They walked in, and Doll glanced out the window at the sun setting.

"This is so beautiful. I'm going to love watching the sunset every evening." Doll walked over to the window and watched the sun go down.

"I know … I knew you would like it." Jordin walked behind her and put his arms around her waist. He then started placing soft kisses on her neck. Doll closed her eyes and enjoyed the feeling.

"So do you like the house?" Jordin asked as he caressed her stomach where his hands were placed as he continued to kiss her neck.

"Yes, I love it. I can't wait to decorate," Doll said in a soft tone with her eyes still closed.

The way Jordin was kissing on her neck, she could hardly speak. His hands were too close to her pelvis, and she was horny as hell. She knew he had to be just as horny because she had him wait for her for so long. Jordin had proven himself in so many ways. He let everyone know that she was his, and if anyone were to mess with her, he had something deadly for them. That was why he wanted to move her far away. After getting shot in his own neighborhood, he felt like his name was buzzing too much for his lady to be left in the city alone while he worked. A lot was going on in his life, and the last thing he needed was his wife to be a target.

"Jordin, I want to feel you inside of me. I've made you wait, and now I'm ready," Doll said in almost a begging tone as she felt his hard dick rubbing against her backside. She knew he was ready too, and she was ready to please him. She wasn't a virgin and knew how to please a man, so she knew he would be satisfied.

Jordin started slowly pulling up her tight skirt. He couldn't wait until he got her into the home so he could give her every inch of him. He had done as right as he could to Doll, and she had taken notice. After getting her skirt up her waist, Doll bent over and arched her back while holding on to the window seal. Jordin dropped his jeans, and his stick came out the peephole of his Calvin Klein boxers. Doll reached behind herself and stroked his dick while he slid her white, lace thong to the side. Doll thought he was big, and she knew he was going to feel good inside of her.

Jordin slid inside of her slowly, causing her to moan. Doll looked back at him as he stroked her slow. He was tall, at least six five, so the way he hovered over her five-foot-five frame turned her on.

"Damn, baby. You are creaming all over my dick. I want you to ride me," Jordin said as he watched his dick go in and out of her. He knew he was going to enjoy having sex with Doll all the time.

He pulled out of her and lay on the floor. Doll slipped out of her dress and watched as Jordin gazed at her body. This was the first time he had seen her naked. Her body was perfect, and he loved how her breasts were so perky. He couldn't wait to put his mouth over them. Doll slid down on his pole and rode him slowly while he played with her nipple.

"Ohh, Jordin, I love you, baby." Doll moaned out as she rotated her hips on his pelvis.

Jordin was loving the way she was bouncing up and down on his dick. He could tell from the way she rotated her hips that he wasn't going to have to teach her anything about pleasing him. Doll got off him and, surprisingly, wrapped her lips around his dick. She wanted to show him that she was good in the oral department so he wouldn't have to go anywhere else. Jordin watched her play with her pussy while she deep throated him.

"Damn, baby, you love me like that?" Jordin asked as he bit on his bottom lip. She was pleasuring him so good he almost couldn't believe it.

"Yup, I sure do. You're my man, and I want to be the only one to please you." She continued to go to work.

The way Doll was sucking on him made his dick throb; he was ready to bust, but he wanted to cum inside of her.

"Lay on your side. That's my favorite position," Jordin said as he stroked his dick.

Doll rolled over on her side, and Jordin slid back inside of her. He gripped her ass as he stroked her slowly. He turned her to face him and started sucking on her titties. Doll moaned. He was making her feel so good. It had been three years since she's had sex. She played with toys, but there was nothing like the real thing.

"Oh my God, Jordin, you are hitting my spot!" Doll cried out.

He covered her lips with his and picked up his pace. Doll bit on his bottom lip, and that turned him into a beast. He started pounding her pussy, causing her to shout.

"Oh, Jordin, I'm about to cum," Doll wept. She had tears forming in her eyes from the pleasurable pain.

"I'm about to bust too," Jordin said, almost out of breath. Jordin was groaning while Doll was moaning. A few strokes later, they both were cumming together.

After Jordin caught his breath, he sat up and started to stand up, but Doll grabbed his arm as she played with her wet kitty. Her body was craving for more.

"Where you going, baby? Let me get you back hard so we can fuck again," Doll begged. Her hormones were at an all-time high.

"We got to hit the road to Laughlin, baby. When we get to our suite, you can have some more of this dick." He smirked and started swinging his hard dick. He knew his sex game was great, and he knew she would be craving more.

Doll laughed. "Okay, babe. I love your ass so much. I hope the honeymoon never ends," Doll said as Jordin helped her off the floor.

Jordin took her into his arms and held her tight. "I love you too, babe."

The two kissed. They then got dressed and headed to pack so they could head to their honeymoon vacation.

CHAPTER TWO

No Mercy...

Four years later...

$\mathcal{J}$ordin sat in the driver's seat of his black-on-black Challenger RT with his pistol on his lap. He was angry, and he didn't understand why niggas loved to test him. It was six in the evening, and the sun was starting to set. Murder and revenge crossed his demonic mind, and it had been a long time since he had to personally take a nigga off the planet. He was loyal to everyone he did business with, yet someone always tried to pull a fast one on him. Therefore, he was done playing games with niggas, and he was ready to set the record straight. Jordin pulled on his blunt as he looked out his passenger window at the house he had been sitting in front of for three hours.

"Three fuckin' hours. I'm about to run in this nigga's shit. Fuck his family," Jordin mumbled to himself as he cocked his gun back and proceeded to exit his car.

Jordin sat his pistol in his passenger seat while he slid on his black hoodie. He wasn't going to mask up, because he wanted the nigga to see who killed him.

"I'm killing everybody. I don't care if it's the nigga kids," Jordin muttered as he exited the car.

Not even trying to hide his piece, he walked up to the door of the two-story house that was in San Bernardino, California, and rang the bell. After a few seconds, the door flew open. It was a tall woman dressed in a yellow sundress. Her curly red hair was all over her head, and she was holding a glass of wine.

"May I help you?" the woman asked with a slight attitude. She hated when people popped up at her house unannounced. It gave her an instant attitude.

"Yeah, you can help me, bitch." Jordin took his gun and shot the woman between her eyes. Her eyes opened wide, and she fell to the floor. Jordin was covered in blood from shooting her at close range. But blood never bothered him at all. Jordin stepped over her body and walked into the home, closing the door.

"Yo, babe, what the fuck was that?" Jordin heard his prey ask from the living room.

Jordin stood there, waiting until they were face to face. When his enemy walked into the living room, he froze when he saw the man he had been dodging for three months. He owed Jordin 20K, and Jordin wanted it, or he wanted his soul as a payment.

"It's me, you hidin' ass nigga. Where the fuck my 20K at?" Jordin asked in a gritty tone as he grabbed the guy by his shirt.

His name was Leroy, and he was one of the grimiest niggas that came out of Compton. His whole reason for moving out the county was to get away from all the people he owed. However, he didn't move far enough for Jordin to not find him. Any information he wanted, he got it.

"Awe, man. I know 20K don't mean nothing to you, Mercy. You're a hood millionaire." The man smirked like Jordin was there to play games.

"You're real cute for a nigga with a gun to his head. Where's the safe? I know you got one in here." Jordin cocked his gun back

"It's in ya mama's pussy, you bitch ass nigga!"

Jordin laughed. "Oh, you're a comedian, huh? Walk your bitch ass upstairs to your room."

The man was cocky, but he did as he was told. The two walked up the stairs, but before they could walk into his room, Leroy pushed Jordin, almost making him stumble down the stairs.

"Bitch ass nigga, you trying to get away?" Jordin asked with bass in his tone. He was becoming angry, and this man was about to see a side of him that he hadn't released in a long time. The man tried to run past Jordin, but Jordin let his gun go off, hitting him in the leg. The man stumbled down the stairs. Jordin walked down the stairs and saw that the man was in pain from the fall and his gunshot wound. He bent down and smirked in Leroy's face, and the man spat at him, letting a ball of spit hit Jordin's shoulder.

"Fuck you, nigga. I don't owe you shit!" Leroy shouted.

"Oh, you don't, huh? Okay." Jordin pulled his Swiss blade from his pocket. He then snatched the drawstring from the man's sweats and tied his hands.

"You ain't gonna get away with this shit, Mercy. I promise you!" the man shouted as sweat started pouring from his forehead. Jordin then took his knife and ran it slowly across the man's neck, enjoying the sight of his blood. The man started to shake from the veins in his neck that were slit wide open.

"Die slow, nigga. Die slow," Jordin said as he watched dude bleed to death from his neck.

Jordin walked up stairs and walked into the man's room. He first went into Leroy's master bedroom and washed the blood from his hands. After he washed his hands, he slid his gloves on that he had in his pocket, prepared to not leave any fingerprints at the crime scene he'd created. He searched the room and finally found the man's safe. He decided to get it open when he got back to the city. Jordin ran out the house and headed to his car. He had to get back to the suburbs to take his wife to work. He looked at the time on his dashboard, and it was six thirty in the evening.

"She's going to kill me like I just did these niggas," Jordin said as he drove off at full speed, looking for the freeway like he hadn't killed two people …

CHAPTER THREE

No love in this home...

*D*oll sat in the window of the suburban home she shared with Jordin. He was forty-five minutes late taking her to work for the second time that week. She thought for sure she was going to be fired with the way he was so careless with picking her up, and she contemplated on taking the bus or calling an Uber. However, Jordin was determined to pick her up and take her to work like a husband should, but he was slacking. Jordin slacked on a lot of things, and she didn't understand why he even married her.

She felt like he had only taken her off the market because he couldn't see her happy with someone else; however, she was miserable with him. She hated that she was so miserable because she was so dedicated to him. Everything she did, she did it for him. He didn't want her hanging with her friends in the club, and he didn't want her leaving the house without him. He was controlling, and it was starting to become unbearable. She wanted to leave him, but every time he felt like she was being distant, he did something to pull her back in. Then he was back to his old ways.

Doll sighed. "I gotta get the fuck out this relationship before I die of misery," Doll said as she still gazed out the window.

At that moment, she finally saw Jordin pulling in front of the house. She grabbed her bag for work and her lunch and headed out the door. Doll had so much attitude built inside from waiting, and she knew it showed all over her face. She knew Jordin hated when she had an attitude, but today, she just didn't care. When she got into the car, she tossed her bag in the backseat, and put on her seatbelt. She had nothing to say to Jordin. She just wanted to get to work, do her twelve-hour shift, and go back home. She knew Jordin would pick her up from work, late as usual, and then she would be stuck at home, sleeping or surfing the web. She thought that was so boring, but she was accustomed to it and couldn't wait to get back home to her boring life.

Jordin looked over at his wife and immediately knew she was angry with him. The creases in her forehead showed it all, and the way her succulent lips poked out gave it all away.

"Something wrong?" Jordin asked as if he had no clue that he was late.

"Yeah, something is wrong, Jordin! You know I have to be at work at six thirty, and you are here at almost seven thirty. Why are you always so late? What the fuck are you doing before you come get me?" Doll asked in a trembling tone, trying to hold back her tears. She was livid at his nonchalant tone and irresponsible ways. It hurt her feelings how he always put her second, and she was starting to think he was doing it on purpose.

"You know what the fuck I be doing, Doll. And I'm sorry for being late. Shit got crazy at the shop, so it caused me to be late. It won't happen again, I promise."

"Whatever ... Just take me to work."

Jordin heard the trembling in her voice, and he felt bad. As tough as he was, Doll knew how to tug at his heart. He knew he had been neglecting his relationship, and the thought of it made him want to change. But his life was crazy. However, Doll was his peace of mind and escape from the streets. He didn't know what he would do if he lost her because of his dishonesty.

Jordin stepped out of his car and walked over to the passenger side. He opened the door and took Doll's hands into his, making her get out of the car, but Doll didn't move. She pushed his hand away and stared out the front window, continuing to keep her tears to herself. She wanted Jordin to be there for her and comfort her, but it made her angry that he only did it when he knew he had fucked up.

"Get out the car, Doll. We're going in the house so we can talk," Jordin said as he continued to try and get her to step out of the car. But she constantly refused.

"I have to go to work, Jordin. You know I can't be late anymore or miss any more days, and here I am, late again. I don't want my degree to go to waste because of you." Doll's tears finally began to fall.

"I don't even know why you go into work anyways, babe. I know you don't want your degree to go to waste, but I can take care the both of us, and you know that. Why won't you just let me take care of you full time? And if you get bored at home, you can come work my counter like you always do," Jordin said in a sympathetic tone.

Doll looked at him with evil eyes. She felt like Jordin was twisting around what she was initially mad at. She didn't want to stay at home, because she knew she would always be stuck while Jordin ran the streets. She didn't want Jordin in the streets anymore. When she met Jordin, he promised her the world and told her he was a businessman. But after she found a key of cocaine in the trunk of his car, his secret was revealed.

"You're missing the fucking point, Jordin! You're always fucking late to pick me up! Are you fucking somebody else?" Doll shouted.

"Like cheating? You're talking crazy, babe. You know I'm not cheating on you. With the shop staying open twenty-four hours now, I'm always needed. I would never cheat on you. Let's just go in the house so we can talk, please." He grabbed her hands again and cuffed them in his. He wanted Doll to believe him, and he didn't want her thinking he was cheating.

"I'm not falling for that tonight. I'm not missing work for you to keep doing the same shit. I don't even know if our relationship is solid enough for me to leave my job and be full time with you. We'll talk tomorrow." She took her hands out of his cuff and proceeded to close the door.

Jordin sighed and got back into the car. He started his engine and got into route to Compton. He knew he was messing up bad, and he knew he had to fix it. He knew he had to get his priorities in order before he lost the best thing that had happened to him. He was only twenty-eight, and he didn't know how to be a husband like he thought he knew how. As much as he loved Doll, he felt like marriage was too much commitment. But he never expressed that to her, because he still wanted to be with her. He had to be whatever Doll wanted him to be, and that was a loving husband that came home at the end of the work day and took his wife to work on time. Not out, doing his dirt.

The car ride was silent the whole twenty-five-minute drive. Jordin exited the 105 Freeway and drove down Compton Ave. until he hit 120th street where Martin Luther King hospital was located. He pulled in front of the emergency entrance and unlocked the doors.

"I promise I'll be on time tonight. I love you, aight?" Jordin said as he gazed at his beautiful wife. She was nothing like the hood girls he was around daily in his shop and on the block. She was different. She was natural, and her caramel skin was flawless. The only thing she didn't wear natural was her auburn twenty-four-inch lace front she wore as a protective style for her long, brown, natural hair. Doll was five feet six and weighed 140 pounds. She was thick in all the right places and made sure she worked out and didn't eat too much junk food. Jordin loved that about her, and he knew if she left him, he wouldn't find anyone else like her. That was why he kept her tucked like his pistol. Nobody could have her.

"Yeah, you better. And for the record, I'm getting a car. I won't need you too much longer." She grabbed her bag from the back seat and exited the car, leaving her words lingering.

She knew he would take her saying she wouldn't need him to offense. Jordin hated when she showed signs that she didn't need him. But the truth was, she didn't. She was in a relationship with him for love and not what he could do for her. Doll always had her goals set out because she never wanted to depend on a man, even if it was her husband. But had he been a good husband, she might have started a home business. But Jordin was not promised, so she continued to work her career in the hospital.

Doll walked into the emergency room and walked behind the double doors that led to the back where all the patients were seen. She rushed quickly down the hall and to her small office she had to herself. When she walked into her office, there were a stack of patient charts with labs that needed to be read, and there also was a pink post-it-note on her desk. She picked it up and read it.

You're late again, for the fifth time this month. See me in my office when you get here – Lena.

"Shit," Doll said and walked out the office to find her supervisor, Lena. Lena was the head supervisor of the billers on her floor, and she did not play about her workers being late. She took her job seriously, and she wanted everyone in her unit to do the same. Lena was a sixty-year-old woman with two years left before she retired. She thought Doll was a hard-working woman when she finally decided to come to work, but that went unnoticed with all her tardiness. Doll had done so much to get to where she was, and here she was, letting a man strip that away from her. She never thought Jordin would ever neglect her because they hit it off hard in the beginning. But as time went by, he started to stray.

"Mrs. Porter, I see you finally made it to work. Let's head to my office so we can have a little chat," Lena said when she ran into Doll in the hallway.

"I'm sorry I'm late again. It won't happen again. I promise. I'll be getting a car and no longer need rides," Doll said, trying to plead her case as they walked into Lena's office. Lena sat behind her desk and picked up a document that was sitting on her desk. She put her glasses on and picked up her pen.

"I hope you won't be late anymore, because I am putting you on a ninety-day probation. That means no tardiness and no leaving early. You are to be here on time every day for ninety days. And if you don't, I'm going to have to let you go. I hate to do it, but rules are rules. I can't let you slide, because everyone else will want that treatment. I thought you were working toward becoming a supervisor in the lab?" Lena asked as she slid Doll her paperwork to sign.

"I am, Lena. But things are so hard right now." Doll put her head down.

"Look, I know things happen in life that we sometimes can't control. But if you want to move up around here, you're going to have to put your personal life to the side and focus on your career." She slid the ninety-day contract to Doll.

Doll was so livid that she was getting put on probation because of Jordin. Every time she thought about it, she thought about something negative. She knew Jordin purposely broke down her car so he could control her every move. When she graduated from college and started working, she would pop up to his shop on her breaks or look for him in her old complex hanging with his boys. She was his wife, so she felt like she could pop up when she felt like it. But after the frequent popups, her car suddenly stopped working.

She signed her name and shook her head.

"Thank you for not firing me, Lena. My job is my life, so I am going to strengthen up," Doll promised.

"Alright, Dollaysia, now get to work. You will be in the lab tonight, so suit up after you go through those labs I sat on your desk." She stood from her desk.

Doll smiled. "I'm on it."

Doll walked out and sighed. She was so glad she wasn't fired on the spot. She was cleaning up her act and putting her foot down with Jordin. She was no longer letting him control her life. She walked into her office and called Breann while she worked on labs. She needed to vent before her long shift ahead of her.

CHAPTER FOUR

The Eastside of Compton No Loyalty...

*B*reann sat on her couch, looking at her kids play in front of the TV while she waited for her best friend, Doll, to call. Every day while Doll was at work, she would call her and talk for hours. Doll's job wasn't hard. She was a lab tech but spent most her shifts in her office, going over everything that was done in the lab in the emergency room. Therefore, she had a lot of downtime while doing the nightshift. Breann didn't work, so she had nothing but time to talk to Doll.

"What's up, boo? What took you so long?" Breann joked as she stood up to pick up her twin boys and take them into their room.

"Girl, Jordin is what took me so long. I was in the office with my boss, trying to save my ass. They put me on a ninety-day probation," Doll said in a bitter tone.

Breann shook her head as she put her twins in their playpen and turned on their TV.

"Girl, his ass was late again, huh? I don't know why you don't have a car. Listening to Jordin say he will take you everywhere sounds like some bullshit to me. It's been a year since your car broke down, and you haven't got another one. I know y'all got the money to afford two cars." Breann walked back into her living room and grabbed her ashtray and lighter. She picked up the blunt that she had waiting for her in her ashtray and lit it.

"Girl, I've been holding on to all my checks since Jordin takes care of everything. I have enough money to buy myself three cars."

"Well, you are slipping. You need to start doing you again because clearly, he does him. I hate that double standard shit. Janario knows not to even play me like that." Breann pulled on her blunt.

"You're right, best friend. I'm almost thirty, no kids, and my man still deals cocaine. I don't know why he doesn't just run his weed shop and leave that white alone."

"It's because there's still money flipping that white girl to these out-of-state niggas as well as that legal green."

"Well, I'm sick of it. Sometimes, I just don't know where we went wrong. We were so close; now he just neglects me. Is he over there with Janario now? I'm sure he went straight there after dropping me off."

Breann glanced into her kitchen and saw Janario and Jordin sitting at her kitchen table, counting money that Janario had gotten from a cross-state run. Jordin had a girl sitting on his lap, drooling over every dollar he counted. She knew her best friend's husband was a cheater, and she felt bad that she kept it from Doll because she knew her friend was a good woman. However, Janario demanded that she stayed out their affairs. Janario and Jordin were best friends, and every time he showed up, he was with the same female, and it wasn't Doll. She couldn't wait until her best friend found out about her man's infidelities.

"Yup, he's here …"

"Well, I'll talk to you tomorrow. I can't even be on the phone. I'm working the lab tonight, and I heard it's busy," Doll said in a bitter tone.

"Okay, girl. Let's go out tomorrow. You need it. I'll ask that bitch Jordin myself," Breann said as she eyed Jordin in the kitchen.

"Yeah, good luck with that," Doll laughed. "But take a drive to my house tomorrow. I'm off. Bring the twins."

"Yeah, we will see …"

The two dismissed their call.

Breann sat her blunt in her ashtray and walked into the kitchen. She stood in the doorway and watched Jordin and Janario run money through their money machines while they made small talk and smoked a blunt. Tiffany was now sitting next to him, rolling another blunt for them. Breann looked at Tiffany and rolled her eyes. She knew she was Jordin's little hood side chick no matter how much he tried to fake like she wasn't. Breann was ready to rip her cheap lace front from her head. She was trashy and nothing like Doll. But she saw why Jordin kept her around.

Doll smoked, but she didn't roll her own blunts. Doll wasn't a hood girl, but Tiffany was from the same hood as him and worshipped the ground Jordin walked on. She would stuff a brick of cocaine in her pussy if Jordin asked her to. She would do anything for him and always considered herself his main lady, knowing he was with Doll. But after he moved Doll out the hood, she hardly visited even though her job was in the heart of his neighborhood.

"What's up, Jordin? I just got off the phone with your wife. She wants to go out tomorrow tonight. You know, live a little, since you do … and you better not say no," Breann crossed her arms and raised her eyebrow.

Jordin and Janario began to laugh.

"Yo, Janario, handle ya girl," Jordin said as he glared at Breann. He knew there was tension between the two.

"Bre, what did I tell you? Didn't I tell you to stay out this man's affairs? It's none of your business. If she wants to go out, tell her to ask Jordin herself. Now go back into the living room. He's about to leave, and I'ma give you some money," Janario said.

"Yeah, nigga, you better give me some money because I don't appreciate this nigga bringing his side hoe into my house while my best friend is at work about to get fucking fired because he can't take his dick out her ass. It's disrespectful as fuck, and I don't want her back in my house!" Breann said firmly as she eyed down Tiffany.

Tiffany turned up her nose and turned around to look at Breann. She had known Breann since middle school, and they never cared too much for each other. Breann knew every whore in the neighborhood, and she knew Tiffany was one of them, looking for a come up off someone else's man.

"Who are you calling a side hoe?" Tiffany had the nerve to say.

"I'm calling you a side hoe, bitch. Don't sit there and act like Mercy is your man, because he ain't. Now hurry up and count y'all money, and get this bitch out my house." Breann walked off, not giving Tiffany a chance to say anything back to her. She walked into the living room, making a dragging sound with her fluffy house slippers and heading to her twin's room.

"Didn't I tell your stupid ass to keep your mouth closed when I bring you over here? You are not supposed to say shit. Let's wrap this shit up so I can take this bitch to her house so she can strap up for this trip," Jordin said with much attitude. He was mad that Tiffany had said something to Breann. He knew they didn't get along, and he knew Breann was holding his secret in and didn't like it. Therefore, he didn't know how long she was going to keep quiet.

A few minutes later, Janario walked into the twin's room to see what his girl and kids were doing. As much as Janario worked with his boy Jordin, he loved his family that he created.

"You need me to take the boys while you take a break?" Janario asked as he walked into the room.

"Yes, I need to go shower and start making you some dinner. But let me ask your ass something, Janario, because you know I don't play that side hoe shit. Do you got another bitch like Jordin has? You better not be out here making me look stupid. You know I'll cut a bitch and you," Breann said as she stood up and handed Janario one of their nine-month-old twins.

"What? You know a nigga ain't cheating. That nigga Mercy's just going through some shit right now. He ain't even fuckin' with ol' girl like that, so you won't have to worry about her anymore. Don't let his actions have you thinking I'm out here fuckin with these bitches, because I'm not," Janario assured her.

"Yeah, okay." Breann walked off and headed to the kitchen to take food out of the freezer. When she walked in, she saw Janario's phone sitting on the table. She gazed at it for a second, debating if she wanted to pick it up. After looking at it for a few seconds, she picked it up. She then punched in his code and started looking through his texts and pictures. She wanted to make sure he was telling the truth. She couldn't lie. Jordin's ways made her paranoid, and she never wanted to be made out of a fool like her best friend. After his phone came up clean, she took a deep breath and sat his phone back on the table.

"I'm glad I got me a good man. I'd kill Jordin's ass if I was Doll," Breann said to herself as she put her pack of meat into the sink.

CHAPTER FIVE

Burnt Bridges

"*You really are starting to hurt my feelings with your neglectful ways. I've contemplated so many times to leave you, and do my own thing. But the love I have for our marriage makes me want to stay and try and work things out. We aren't boyfriend and girlfriend anymore, Jordin. We are married and been married for four years now. I really wish you would consider my job and my sanity like I do yours so we could make this relationship work. We haven't even had sex in two weeks, because you are never home. I only see you when you drop me off and pick me up from work. We need to get back to us, so be on time tonight so we can sort things out. Because if we don't, I'm filing for a separation.*"

Jordin lay back on Tiffany's bed, reading the text he had just gotten from Doll. He felt like a piece of shit, lying up with Tiffany while his wife was begging for his attention. He had been lying to her since the day he made her his girl. He had been messing around with Tiffany for well over seven years. He and Doll had been together for four years. He hadn't told her a lot of things, because he wanted to protect her. Not only was Tiffany his budtender at his weed shop, she also did his cocaine runs across state lines for him. She was something like his ride or die, and Doll was his gem. He was living a double life and becoming tired. He would never have Doll out doing the things he had Tiffany doing, though. He married Doll because he wanted to secure a solid relationship for his future until he deadened his relationship with Tiffany. And her expiration date was coming fast.

He and Tiffany had always kept their relationship a secret for years because Jordin liked it that way due to Tiffany's rep. Everyone in the hood knew Jordin had a wife and fucked with Tiffany, but no one dared to get into his affairs. Therefore, Doll had no clue what was really going on with her husband. Not only did she not know he was cheating, but she also didn't know he was on a killing spree, killing anyone who owed him money.

"You need to tell Janario's baby mama to stop talking shit when I'm around. I don't say shit to her. But I'm going to start," Tiffany said as she sat at the end of the bed in her black thong and lace bra.

"She has a right to say what she wants in her own home. And you know my wife is her best friend, so of course, she doesn't like you. She probably seen you sitting on my lap. You need to stop doing dumb shit," Jordin said in a dry tone as he sat up and set his phone on the nightstand.

"I don't give a fuck, Jordin. You know I'm pregnant with your baby, and I want to be under you," Tiffany said as she scooted closer to Jordin. She was three weeks pregnant, and Jordin didn't like it one bit.

"Don't start that baby shit, Tiffany. I told you what you had to do. We can't have a fucking kid together. After this last run, I'm not fucking with you no more. My wife needs me. You can still work at the shop, but I can't keep fuckin' you."

"You weren't thinking about the bitch when you picked me up as soon as you dropped her off. You also weren't thinking about the bitch when you nutted in me, so don't come at me with the wifey shit because she's giving you a hard time. You told me you loved me and wanted me to have your baby. Now you are changing your mind," Tiffany said in a bitter tone.

"Will you listen to yourself, Tiffany? First off, stop calling her a bitch, and second, you know I was drunk, and you know I didn't nut in you intentionally. The fuckin' condom broke. And the only reason why I picked you up so fast was because you keep blowing up my phone. You need to stop doing that shit."

"Whatever, Mercy." She stood up. "Strap me up so I can get on the road. I'm sick of you and your wife, so if you are done with me, I'm done with your ass too."

Jordin stood up and started taping bags of cocaine to her body with clear duct tape. After he was done taping her up, Tiffany put on her blue Adidas sweat suit, and they both headed out her apartment. As she was getting into her rental car, Jordin grabbed her arm aggressively.

"Get rid of that fuckin' baby, or I will. You got that, Tiffany? I'll fucking kill that baby and you if I have too."

"Fuck you, Mercy. I'll see you when I get back." Tiffany got in the car and slammed the door. She started the car and drove off, not looking twice at Jordin. She was angry he was trying to make her get rid of her baby when she didn't want to.

Jordin, on the other hand, didn't care about her feelings. He never did, and he didn't understand why he was so attached to her. Compared to Doll, she was a scum that didn't amount to him. But her slick talk and get-money ways kept him going back to her. Doll didn't like going to hood parties when Jordin was entitled to attend them when the time came, and Tiffany attended every one of those parties. There was never a time Jordin fucked her when he was sober. He was always drunk, and now he was slipping because she was now pregnant.

"I gotta get rid of this bitch, fast," Jordin said to himself as he got into his truck.

He then drove to his shop and served a few customers until it was time to go pick up Doll. He knew she was hurting, and he knew he had to do something to make up with her. He knew she was tired of the making up just for him to fuck up again. It was even getting old for him. He was tired of telling lies to her. He was tired of telling one lie and telling another to back up his initial lie. His conscience had gotten so bad that he contemplated confessing everything to her, but he knew she would never forgive him.

I'm just going to have to make it up to her, and do right.

He stuffed the stacks of money into his safe and locked it. He left out the back of his shop and headed to his car. He pulled up in front of Doll's job ten minutes early. Five minutes later, Doll had walked out. She was surprised to see him five minutes early, and she was pleased because she was ready to go home.

"What's up, babe? I'm on time like I said," Jordin said as he reached over and kissed her.

"I appreciate that, Jordin. Can we stop and get food and then go home?" Doll asked as she let her seat back and put on her seatbelt.

"We can do whatever you want to do. Norm's or Denny's is the only place open, so call it in, and we can pick it up."

After they picked up their food, they headed home. As soon as they walked into the house, Jordin sat the food down in the kitchen. Without warning, Jordin swept Doll off her feet, startling her.

"Jordin, what are you doing, boy? Put me down," Doll said in an uninterested tone. It was two thirty in the morning, and she wasn't in the mood to be romanced. She knew what he was trying to do, and she wasn't in the mood.

"I want my lady to feel good, so go take your scrubs off so we can take a shower together," Jordin said as he took off his shirt, showing off his long scar from being shot and all his tattoos.

"Jordin, I'm sorry, but I'm really not in the romance mood. I'm tired. Can we try again tomorrow?" Doll asked in a begging tone.

"Well, I'm going to get you in the mood." He started helping her get her scrubs over her head. Jordin couldn't wait until the next day to please her. He felt so bad about his actions that she deserved to be romanced on the spot like he used to do when she came home from work.

After they got out their clothes, they both took a hot, steamy shower together. Jordin didn't let her lift a finger. He lathered up her loofa and started washing her body. Doll was tensed at first, but once he started massaging her as he washed up body, she loosened up a little.

He might be coming around a little. But I'm still not convinced. It's just a shower, Doll thought to herself as he slid her under the water and started rinsing her body.

After they showered, Jordin got out first and wrapped a towel around himself. Then he got Doll's robe for her and wrapped it around her. They both slipped on their night clothes and headed down to the kitchen to eat their food. As they were eating, Jordin was silent, and so was Doll. She had so many thoughts in her head that needed to be answered.

"So why are you always late, Jordin? What's going on when I'm not around? I know you have enough staff to take over, so you can pick me up and come home at night," Doll said, starting their conversation.

Jordin took a bite of his eggs and then chewed them up as he thought about what he was going to tell her. It was eating him up inside, knowing that he had been dishonest, and looking into Doll's eyes was becoming unbearable every time he told a lie. But he knew he had to lie to her if he wanted to keep her.

"I know. I just like running my own business." He shrugged.

"No, the problem is that you are selling dope, Jordin. You're letting your Mercy persona ruin us. Does that bitch Tiffany still like you? I don't know why you even still have her around."

"I don't know what Tiffany likes. She's just my budtender. I don't know how many times I have to tell you that. And as far as me dealing dope, you know the deal. I'm helping Janario out of his situation. I can't let him do this dope shit alone, and you know I'm not letting my nigga go out like that."

"Janario is a grown ass man and owns the shop with you. Why

isn't his money adding up to yours? I just don't get it. I feel like you are lying to me about something."

"Well, I'm not lying to you about anything ..." Jordin stood up and stood in front of Doll. She was looking good in her tank top and boy shorts. Her nipples were visible through her top, and her thick thighs were so tempting.

He then knelt down and opened her legs and ran his fingers up and down her pussy.

"Jordin, I'm eating," Doll said as she looked down at him. She couldn't deny it was feeling good, but she knew he was only trying to take her mind off his wrongdoings.

"I'm eating too," Jordin said with a smirk as he dived face first into her creamy middle. However, her body never rejected Jordin. She dropped her fork and opened her legs, letting Jordin go deeper inside of her with his finger as he licked her clit. She grabbed the top of his head, pushing his face further as she rotated her hips slowly. The way she was rotating her hips had Jordin hard as a rock. He loved when he could make his wife feel good. She was the only woman he went down on, so when he did it, he took advantage and enjoyed it.

"Let's take this to the bedroom," Doll said as she looked down at Jordin eating her like a pink starburst.

Jordin picked her up from her chair and carried her to their bedroom where they made love for the next two hours.

$$$$$

The next morning, Doll woke up feeling a little groggy from going to sleep so late with Jordin. She was glad she didn't have work for the next two days, so she lay back down and closed her eyes.

"Baby, don't go back to sleep. Wake up," Jordin said with a smile on his face as he stood over Doll fully dressed.

"What time is it? My eyes are burning," Doll said as she tried to look around their room.

"It's noon. Get up and get dressed. I want to take you somewhere," Jordin said as he pulled the covers off her slowly.

Doll sat up and stretched. She got out of bed and walked into the bathroom to shower. She took a quick shower, got out, and put on a pair of jeans and a t-shirt. She wasn't in the mood to get dressed up. Once she was ready, she and Jordin headed out. Doll slept their whole twenty-minute ride to the city. She woke up when she felt the car stop. When she opened her eyes, they were at a luxury car dealership in Compton.

"What are we doing here?" Doll asked as she gazed at Jordin.

"I know you are sick of me dropping you off and picking you up, so I want to get you a car. I know you work hard, but I love taking care of you, Doll, so if you want another car, then I'm going to get you one."

"You got me out of bed to take me to buy a car because you knew I was going to do it myself," Doll said, not interested in his alleged good gesture.

"Just let me be your husband like you want me to be and take care of you, babe. Why do you give a nigga such a hard time when I try and do good?"

"Because you are only trying to do good when you know you are on my bad side. I don't want a car. I want you to be on time and come home at night, Jordin. I don't want material things; I want you."

Jordin sighed. He knew she was right, and he knew that was what she really wanted. He knew showering her with gifts was getting old, especially since she had her own money to spend. But that was the only thing he knew to do to please her.

"Just let me buy you whatever you want off this lot, and I promise I'm going to come around. Can you just trust in me, please?"

"Promises, promises … I already see something I like, so let's go see what they are talking about," Doll said as she reached for the door to get out.

Before she got out, Jordin grabbed her arm. "Can you at least enjoy this and not have an attitude?"

"Yeah, I can do that …" She pulled her arm away from him and got out.

"My man, Jordin! I see you back to trade in that raggedy Challenger. You drive around here like you're broke now. You used to always buy luxury cars," the salesman said when he walked up to Doll and Jordin. Jordin had been coming to his dealership for years.

"What's up, man? Nah, I'm here buying my wife a car. I told her she can have whatever she wants on this lot, and she said she already knows what she wants," Jordin said as he pulled Doll by her waist and started kissing on her neck like they were a happy couple. Doll played his game as well, so she smiled.

"Yup, I sure do. I think I like that black-on-black Porsche truck sitting up front," Doll said with a smile. She was actually happy that she was finally getting another car, and she was going to make Jordin cash out on the most expensive car the dealer had.

"Well, let's go check it out," the salesman said as escorted them inside the dealer. After they were approved to test drive the truck, Doll was behind the wheel, driving up Compton Blvd., with Jordin in her passenger seat as she test drove her potential whip.

"So do you like this one?" Jordin asked as she made her way back to the dealership.

"Yeah, I like it. Breann is going to be hating," she joked. She couldn't wait to pull up on her best friend in her new truck.

"I bet she is," Jordin said with a smile.

When they got back into the dealership, Jordin paid for her car upfront with cash.

"Thank you for buying me a car, Jordin. This is really going to get me back on track with work, and you don't have to worry about picking me up anymore." She threw her arms around him and kissed him on the lips.

"I told you anything you want, you got it. I know I been fucking up lately, but I really want to make this right."

"I know you do. But we still have a lot to work out. I still have a lot of thinking to do, so go to work, and we can talk about it further later, okay?" Doll said as she looked him in the eyes. She wasn't in the mood to argue or put her foot down about anything. She was having a good day, and she didn't want to ruin it with their problems.

"Alright. Call me when you get home, and I'll make my way there.

Cook a nigga some dinner at least since I cashed out on your fine ass."
He smacked her ass.

"Alright, boy. You just better be home before the food is done."

The two of them went their separate ways ...

CHAPTER SIX

He's just eye candy...

The following night ...

$\mathcal{D}$oll sat at her vanity, listening to Toni Braxton's "Seven Whole Days" as she applied mascara to her eyelashes. After cleaning her house and making Jordin a small dinner, she started getting ready for her night out with Breann. It had been so long since she went out, and she was a little too excited to be out of Jordin's presence. He was trying so hard to keep a smile on her face, and all she could do was fake it. She knew he was only trying to get back on her good side, and it was hardly working. Although his sex had been good for the last couple days, she still was not convinced that he was ready to do better.

She stood up from her vanity and slid on a tight, black dress and pulled out a pair of expensive, open-toe stilettoes. She was going out to have a drink at a lounge with Breann. She was going to make Jordin stay at home and hold his breath until she came home because she had decided to stay at a hotel until morning, and she wasn't letting him know. She knew when Jordin saw her walking out, looking sexy, he

71

would stop her. She knew he would be pissed that she was going out and didn't have him on her side while she was dressed the way she was. He was overprotective. But tonight, she was living by her own rules to teach him that she could live her life without him.

Jordin walked into the room and spotted Doll sliding on her heels. She was looking good enough to eat, and he couldn't wait until she came home tipsy so he could have a piece of her. He loved everything about Doll. She was beautiful, and she was smart. He loved the way she carried herself as a classy woman and made herself available for him when he wasn't fucking up. They were on good terms, and he knew she would lay it on him when she came home.

Jordin walked behind her and wrapped his arms around her waist while she was still bending over, fixing the straps on her stilettos. She then stood up straight once her shoes were adjusted.

"Don't you think that dress is a little too tight? I don't want them niggas drooling over my wife." He kissed her neck.

"Well, if they are drooling, at least I know I still got it." Doll took his hands from around her waist and walked over to her vanity. She started putting everything she needed in her purse.

"Don't play me, Doll. And don't talk to no fuck niggas," Jordin said as he followed her down the hall to their living room. Doll was bad, and Jordin knew it because he felt like he created her with all the expensive clothing he filled her closet with. Everywhere they went, men peeped her out, and he did not like it. But tonight, he was letting her let it all hang out.

"I won't ... I'll make sure he's a boss." She smirked as she switched her ass down the hallway. She knew Jordin's eyes were fixed to her ass, so she put extras on her switch.

"Get fucked up, Dollaysia. And come home tonight. Don't spend a night in Compton with Breann."

"Whatever, nigga." She grabbed her keys from the dining room table and headed out the door. She turned on her R&B playlist in her new truck and headed out her driveway with Jordin standing in the doorway, looking at her.

Jordin reached into his pocket and pulled out his phone. He dialed a number, and the phone started ringing. On the second ring, a man answered the phone.

"Yeah, what up, bro? Did you find out the lounge she is going to be at?" Brian asked.

"Yeah, the Hollywood hookah lounge. Make sure you keep a good eye on her," Jordin stated firmly.

"You got it, boss." Brian hung up the phone.

Jordin smirked and then walked back into the house …

$$$$$

Doll arrived at a small lounge that was in Hollywood, California. She parked in front and stepped out her truck. She handed her keys to valet and headed inside the club. She paid her entry and started looking for Breann. The club was dim and a little bit foggy. Music was playing while the small crowd had drinks while they socialized. A small crowd was the only thing she could deal with. She wasn't too much into rap and hip-hop clubs unless she had to appear with Jordin, so a nice hookah lounge always fulfilled her when she wanted to hit the club scene and have a drink.

Finally making her way to the back of the club, she spotted Breann sitting in a VIP section. She was already puffing on a hookah pipe, blowing out huge clouds of smoke. She was wearing a dark-blue lace front wig that was pulled up in a bun with shades covering her eyes.

"Hey, girl, I finally made it," Doll said as she walked into the section.

"What's up, bitch? You got me in this boring ass lounge. Let's hurry up and order a bottle so we can liven this thing up," Breann said as she picked up the liquor menu.

"You know this is the only scene I fuck with. You know I won't go anywhere else unless it's with Jordin." She shrugged.

"I know ... And you're the only bitch that can drag me to a dull ass hookah bar with these white folk and cornball niggas. But what's up with you? I haven't talked to you since the night you went to work."

Doll picked up one of the hookah stems. "That nigga Jordin has been making up to me for a couple days now. He's been licking up and down my ass, literally. He bought me a new truck because he knew I was going to go out and buy my own car. I was going to pull up on you, but I decided not to since I don't want nobody over there to know what I'm riding in. I still feel like I'm mad at him, though. He just irks me now with that late bullshit. I love him, but he gets on my nerves enough to leave him until he gets his shit together." Doll pulled on her hookah stem and blew out smoke. She couldn't even believe what she was saying. She had never spoken out loud about leaving Jordin, but she felt like it was coming.

"Oh, wow … Is it that bad?" Breann asked.

"Yes, girl. More and more every day. It's like when he makes up to me now, it's fake. Have you heard anything about him in the streets? I asked him if he was cheating, and he said no."

"I haven't heard anything about him. You know Jordin got these niggas and bitches on hush when it comes to his business." Breann hated that she had to lie to Doll in her face. She so badly wanted to tell her about Tiffany, but she knew Janario would be upset. Janario had a temper when it came to people getting in his affairs, and Janario would rather his girl stayed out the madness. He didn't want anything happening to her, so Breann kept her mouth closed.

"I'm just tripping at the fact that he doesn't tell me too much about why he has been late and not coming home. He needs to leave the damn drug shit alone; I do know that."

"Damn… I'm so sorry you feel like that, but look at the bright side … Everyone knows he is married to you. I know you love Jordin, but Mercy is what's hot in the streets. You've been knowing he was in this shit 'til death, and you chose to live life with him. You're not going to get that nigga off the streets, though, so if you gonna leave him, you might as well do it," Breann stated. She always gave Doll raw advice just like she gave her.

She had known Jordin longer than Doll, and she was still in the streets herself at times. She knew that they were making cross-state runs dealing dope in Vegas and in the south. They were bringing in thousands, and she knew all this information because they counted their dope money at her place and stashed it. They kept their illegal money separate from their legal money. She felt for her best friend. But she knew like everyone else he was addicted to the streets.

"Yeah … Well, when he is dead and gone, that money won't mean a thing, so he needs to get his shit right. Now where the fuck is this waiter?" Doll asked, not really wanting to talk about her relationship anymore. She hated how everyone around her was so street driven while she focused on legit goals. True, Jordin had a legit business and hadn't been caught, because the city knew he ran a weed shop. But Doll knew that was his shield from the police.

"Just check his phone, girl. That's what I do to get my information." She shrugged.

At that moment, two men walked up to their section. The girls looked at the men and smiled. They were two black guys. They were tall and looked built. They were also sexy in the face. They were dressed casual and decent.

"Excuse me, I believe you are sitting in our section," one of the men said as he gazed at Doll.

"No, this is ours. We reserved it earlier today with the owner via text," Doll responded.

"Well, all the other sections are taken with big parties, and we were told this was the one we reserved, so could we just share? It's only us two. We're not trying to sit at the bar."

"How do we know you paid to sit in here and not trying to spoof us? We need to see some kind of receipt," Breann shot at the men.

She wasn't really in the mood for extra company even though they were cute. She knew they were squares, and she liked *hood niggas* like Janario …

One of the men reached into his pocket and pulled out a wad of cash and showed it to the women. "I don't have to *spoof* you, lil' mama. I got money; that's my receipt."

Doll and Breann laughed. "Well, alright, *baller*. I guess drinks are on y'all then," Doll said.

"Drinks ain't nothin'. I can buy you a house if I wanted," one of the guys said in a cocky tone to Doll.

At first, Doll and Breann thought they were squares and two gym rats. But they had swag, and they had money. One guy sat on the side of Doll, and his friend sat next to Breann.

"So what's y'all names? Y'all kind of cute," Breann said to the men.

"My name is Donni, and this is my boy, Jap," Donni said, introducing himself and his friend. Donni was sitting next to Doll, and he was digging her features.

"Jap? Why they call you Jap?" Breann questioned.

"Because I have tight eyes like I'm Japanese," he chuckled.

"Well, my name is Bre, and this is my girl, Doll."

After their introductions, their waiter finally came over and took their order. Before they knew it, they were halfway done with a jug of orange juice and champagne. They were talking, cracking jokes, and having a good time. They were pretty much strangers to each other, but they felt like they had known each other for a long time with the good time they were having.

"Let's dance a little bit, bitch. We both have to drive, and I know you're twisted," Breann said as she stood over Doll.

Doll found herself having a good time with Donni. He was cute, and he wasn't thirsty. They were having a nice conversation about business and her job. He owned a couple gyms and called himself a celebrity trainer. Doll thought that was cool because she was into fitness as well.

Doll stood up and excused herself from Donni. She and Breann then walked to the dance floor and started dancing to the music together. Doll could feel herself working up a sweat, which was good because that meant the liquor was coming out her pores.

"Can I dance with you, little lady?" Donni walked up and asked from behind Doll. She could already feel him dancing on her, so she started grinding on him just a little bit.

"Yeah, but keep your hands to yourself. I'm married." She flashed her huge diamond ring over her shoulder.

"That doesn't bother me at all." He grabbed her waist and pulled her closer.

The two danced to the alternative R&B song while Doll went into deep thought. She knew Jordin would probably kill Donni if he saw him grinding on her. To Jordin, she was his gem, and he didn't want anyone getting close to her. She hadn't had a man touch her in years, and for Donni to be close to her felt good since Jordin wasn't around. She felt free, and she was glad to know men were still attracted to her. Doll felt Donni's hands slowly going up her thigh. She was stunned to feel his hand caress her thigh, so she moved away.

"Alright, Donni. I think I'm sobered up. I'll see you around," Doll said as she proceeded to walk off.

"Well, can we exchange numbers? I enjoyed my night with you. Maybe we can train together," he smiled.

Doll looked him over again. He was handsome, and his sexy chocolate skin was looking good enough to taste. True, she was planning to leave Jordin if he didn't change his ways. But she wasn't ready to entertain another man. Especially with Jordin still in her life and being so possessive.

"I'll catch you on the rebound, Donni. Have a nice night."

She walked off and grabbed Breann so they could leave at the same time. As they waited for valet to bring their cars, Breann looked over at Doll.

"I saw the way you and ol' boy were vibing. Do you like him?" Breann asked with a smirk on her face.

"Girl, I only knew the nigga two hours. We were hardly vibing."

"Yeah, right. But you better get yo' side nigga. Jordin's ass better watch out!" Breann said loudly as she laughed.

"You're crazy, Bre. You know Jordin will kill any side nigga I get."

Valet finally brought their cars, and the girls went their separate ways. Doll looked at the time and saw that it was one in the morning. Jordin had called her a few times, but she did not call him back. She knew he was still awake and probably mad that she wasn't answering her phone, so she decided to go to a hotel for the night. She really didn't want to be in his presence while she had liquor in her system. She needed some time to think about what she was going to do with her husband. They were on good terms, but she knew she had to lay down the law. She knew she had to give him an ultimatum.

Doll parked in the parking structure and grabbed her purse. She checked into her room and wasted no time getting on the elevator. All she could think about was resting her eyes. She walked into her cozy, luxury room at the W hotel. She slipped off her heels and her dress. She walked into the restroom and cleaned up before climbing into the comfy bed. When she came out, she grabbed the remote to the TV and lay down. As she surfed the channels, she thought about what she was going to do with Jordin. Whatever was making him late and keeping him out for days, he was going to have to quit it because if he didn't, she was leaving him and not looking back.

$$$$$$

Doll tiptoed through her foyer at five in the morning. She had forgotten that she couldn't stay at her hotel all day because she had to meet with Jordin since she promised to work his counter while Tiffany was out. She was so tired, but she knew once she took a shower and made some green tea, she would be wide awake for the day. She knew Jordin was home, but she figured he probably would be sleep. When she walked through the living room, she felt Jordin grab her arm and push her onto the couch.

"You and Breann's hoe asses went to the club to meet up with some niggas! Where the fuck you been all night? You been with that nigga you were dancing with, huh? You think I don't have eyes? You think I don't know your every move like you know mine? Did you fuck him!" Jordin asked aggressively as he pinned her to the couch.

Once Doll left the house, he had one of his workers follow her to the lounge and keep an eye on her while she was there. He only sent them to make sure she had protection. But when his goon sent a video of her dancing with another man, his jealousy was at an all-time high.

"Get the fuck off me! Have you been up all night, waiting for me, you creep! We didn't meet up with anybody!" she shouted as she struggled to get him off her. But his hold was tight. She hated when Jordin got aggressive with her when she didn't do things his way.

"Yeah, I've been up all night. I've been waiting for your stupid ass! You trying to leave me, Doll? Huh, you wanna leave?"

"Yes, I want to leave! You don't take care of home, and you're still running the streets and being a damn criminal while I'm always in this damn house. You think I want to live like this? Always living in fear and wondering when my man is coming home?" She squirmed to get out his hold, but she still didn't have any luck.

"You chose to live in fear, what the fuck! I always make sure you are protected. You think some square ass buff nigga is going to protect you?" He let her arms go and reached under her skirt. "Take your fucking panties off. I want to see if you fucked that nigga."

"I'm not taking anything off! Let me go!" she shouted as she struggled to get out his hold.

Jordin reached under her skirt with one hand, and she didn't have on any underwear. "You don't have any fucking panties on! You fucked him?" Jordin asked with an evil look on his face. He was crushed at the thought that his wife was cheating.

As soon as he let her arms go, she mushed his face so hard that he fell off her. She sprinted to their room and slammed the door. She locked it and sat on the bed.

"Open this fuckin' door, or I'm going to kick it down!" Jordin shouted as he banged on the door. He was angry, and he didn't want Doll to leave. He loved her, and she was his backbone to anything that secured them a future. He needed her and didn't know what he would do without her.

"No, because I'm sick of you always trying to butter me up when your ass is doing wrong. I didn't have sex with anyone, and you know that! So go start your day, Jordin. Use the guest room and bathroom."

Boom!

Jordin kicked in the bedroom door, knocking it off the hinges. Doll tried to sprint to the bathroom, but Jordin yet again caught her. He pinned her arms down again, but he started kissing on her neck. He loved Doll, and he wasn't going to let her leave him. He was her protector, and he wasn't going to let another man come in and replace what he'd been lacking.

"Stop, Jordin. Let me go. I don't want to do anything with you." Doll was trying to fight him off, but he continued to kiss her neck and nibble on her ear. He was turning her on, and it made her so angry because she knew he was going to leave her feeling defeated yet again. Her body was craving her husband no matter how much she tried to fight him off. He slid down and pulled her shirt up with one hand while he still had her hands pinned with one of his hands. He started sucking on her nipples and flicking them with his tongue.

"I love you, Dollaysia Marae Porter. I love everything about you," Jordin said in a low, seductive tone as he played with her nipples. The sensation was sending vibrations to her clitoris that she could no longer dismiss.

Doll loved everything about him too. She loved how tall he was, and she loved his deep, caramel-colored skin. He had a beautiful smile that she loved, and his dimples made her blush every time he showed them off to her. She loved how he made her feel protected and made her feel special when they were finally living like a husband and wife should. Nonetheless, she didn't speak her feelings to him. She was still mad, and she wasn't going to give up about him becoming a better husband. She was ready to get off birth control and start a family but not while he was in the position he was in. She was ready to give him an ultimatum and make him choose her or the streets. However, she wasn't going to tell him anything until he finished pleasing her.

After Jordin pleased her on their bedroom floor, Doll stood up from the floor and headed for the shower with Jordin in tow. She turned on the shower while he stood at the bathroom sink, preparing to brush his teeth. She stepped inside the steaming water and ran her head under it. She started thinking about her ultimatum she had come up with for Jordin, and she was ready to let him know.

"I just want to let you know that I have been doing a lot of thinking. I'm ready to start a family, and I want you to become a real husband. I'm not your trap queen; I'm your wife, so you have ninety days to get your shit together, or I am filing for separation until you do."

There was a brief silence in the restroom. Doll was waiting for him to flip out again, but Jordin thought about every word she said. He could agree that he was ready to start a family. He was almost thirty, and he was the only one in his squad that didn't have any kids other than the one Tiffany was carrying. Janario had two children, and he took care of each one of them while still living his street life. He understood why Doll wanted him off the streets, but he was in too deep. There was a lot he had to take care of before he just stepped off his throne. But he knew he had to agree to what she was asking for. He didn't want to lose her. Therefore, he was going to try his hardest to step down and become an honest man for Doll.

"You got it, sweetheart. Ninety days ... And I'll make sure to get the door fixed," Jordin said as he brushed his teeth.

"Yeah, you do that."

Nothing else was said. The two got dressed and started their day of money making ...

CHAPTER SEVEN

One week Later...

 iffany had finally come back from Vegas doing her run for Jordin. She had stayed an extra couple of days to get her mind right from the shit she was going through with Jordin. She thought he was a bitch for trying to make her get rid of her baby. This was the first time she had ever been pregnant, and she was already attached to her fetus. She was to the point that she didn't care if Jordin didn't want to be in her and her baby's life. She knew she could take care of her baby without him regardless of how he felt.

She knew for a long time that Jordin cared nothing for her anymore. The sex they had, there was no feelings attached, and the money he gave her was only for a job well done in the field. She knew his heart was with Doll, but her envy caused her to keep making Jordin pursue her. She knew she was nothing like Doll, and it made her angry. Tiffany didn't even have a legit high school diploma, while Doll had a degree and a solid career.

Tiffany sighed and stepped out of her rental car. She wanted to shower and change before Jordin came to pick up the money she had collected. Usually, she would try and convince him to stay at her house, but today, she just wanted to give him his money so he could go on about his day. The baby she was carrying had her tired and sick to her stomach. She couldn't wait until she was done with her first trimester so her sickness could go away.

As she was opening her apartment door, she saw Jordin pulling into the parking lot. He rolled his window down, and a cloud of smoke came seeping out. "Get in the car, let's take a ride," Jordin said as he hit the locks on the door.

"Mercy, I don't feel like it. I just want to go in and shower. Just take your money and go. I'll ride with you later," Tiffany said, trying to sound as tired as she could so Jordin could leave.

"Get your ass over here and get in the car. This isn't up for debate, Tiffany." Mercy blew smoke from his nose like a bull. He was a little upset and had to handle somethings with her. He had ninety days to get right, and the baby Tiffany was carrying was his first elimination.

Tiffany smacked her lips and walked over to his car with the huge Birkin bag she was carrying with his money in it. She got into his passenger and tossed the purse in his lap. He looked in it and saw stacks of money and a brick of coke. He then took out a stack and tossed the bag in the backseat.

"Where are we going?" Tiffany asked as she stared at Jordin, but he didn't say a word. He continued to drive with his music turned up.

Ten minutes later, Jordin pulled into the parking lot of Planned Parenthood. Tiffany looked around, and she immediately became upset when she saw where they were. But Jordin spoke before she did.

He killed his engine. He tossed the stack of money he had taken out her purse into her lap.

"Get rid of that fuckin' baby, Tiffany."

"I'm not getting rid of my baby, Mercy. I swear you ain't shit. You lead me on all these years, and now you just want to get rid of me and my baby!" she shouted with tears streaming from her eyes.

She had never cried over or in front of Jordin, and she felt weak. She knew although she was saying she didn't want to get rid of the baby, she knew she would be doing it anyway. She knew if Jordin had anything to do with killing the baby himself, she would end up dead to.

Jordin reached over and grabbed Tiffany by her throat mid-sentence. He was done playing games with her, and he was going to show her that he was serious.

"I don't want to hear no sob story bullshit, Tiffany. Get your bitch ass out my car and get rid of that baby. I never led you on. You knew from the start I didn't want a fuckin relationship with you, and you made it clear that you didn't want one with me when you started fuckin all my homies on the low like I don't know. I never said I wanted to be with you. You were always a hoe and business to me, so don't sit here and act like we had something when we didn't. I'm moving on with my wife, and I don't want shit to do with you. As a matter of fact, you can't work at my shop no more. This shit is done." Jordin let her throat go.

Tiffany had nothing to say. She was hurt, and she didn't know how to control her emotions. All she felt was hate toward Jordin, and she was really done with him if she wasn't before.

"Fuck you! Go have your little life. But trust me, the truth will come to the light, and she will see what everyone else sees. A man whore and a fucking liar." She opened the door.

"Yeah, yeah … I'll be out here waiting just in case your ass tries to duck off," Jordin said, disregarding her statement.

When she got out the car, Jordin found a parking spot and waited for Tiffany. He laid his seat back and lit his blunt back. He wasn't letting Tiffany out his sight until he knew for sure she had the abortion. He knew Tiffany had been trying to trap him, and he finally slipped up. He started thinking about the first time he encountered Tiffany. When he met her, he thought she was innocent, but once he got to know her and his homies started telling him about her rep, he quickly changed his mind about wifing her. However, he kept her on his team because she would do anything for him no matter who he was fucking on. Jordin closed his eyes, and remember the day he bumped into her …

Mercy was beating the pavement as fast as he could as the LAPD chased behind him on foot. He was getting tired because he had been running nonstop for at least three minutes, and his sagging pants wouldn't stay up. However, he knew he had to push it to the limit if he didn't want to get caught.

Mercy turned the corner on his block after running down a half-mile long alley and kept running. As he was running, he saw a group of neighborhood girls standing in a circle, smoking a blunt, and listening to music. He took notice that one of the girls had a huge purse hanging on her arm. When he got closer, he noticed that her bag was wide open. He took his sack of dope and tossed it in her purse. He kept running and didn't look back. The officers passed up the group of girls like they weren't even standing there. They had been trying to catch up with Mercy for days, so they were not concerned with them outside smoking weed.

The police finally caught up with Mercy and shoved him to the ground.

"I ain't got shit. Y'all fucking with the wrong nigga," Mercy said as they shoved his face into the ground.

"Yeah right, you little drug dealing bastard. We know you have been responsible for all these random killings around here too!" the cop said as he searched Mercy.

"Y'all ain't got shit on me. Y'all gonna have to let me go regardless."

"Shut up." The officer kicked him.

"I'ma sue y'all for police brutality. This is bullshit!"

"I said shut your bitch ass up!" the officer shouted again.

After the police roughed him up some more and continued to search him, they found nothing, so they were forced to let him go even though they were pissed. Mercy made his way back down the street to find the girl he had dumped his sack on. He needed it back so he could continue his mission to sell it.

When he walked up, he heard the girls discussing what had happened. They couldn't believe he had run by and dropped a sack in their friend's purse. She was reaching in for her lip gloss and pulled out his Ziploc package.

"My bad about that. Can I have my shit back, though? The police were on my ass. I had to do something," Mercy said to the girl as she held his sack in her hand.

"*You could have got my girl locked up for this shit, nigga. You're crazy,*" *one of the girls spoke up and said to Mercy.*

"*Yeah, boy. I'm not going down for you,*" *the girl said as she passed him his sack.*

The girl was Tiffany, and little did he know, Tiffany had been crushing on him for a while. She had been with a couple of his friends, but she wanted Mercy in the worse way. She knew everything about him and would do anything to get in his jeans. She was happy he had come back for his sack because she wanted to see his face again.

"*My bad, lil' mama. I can shoot you some cash later if you come to my house. I'm sure y'all know where I live,*" *Mercy said as he stuffed his sack in his socks.*

"*Yes, we know where you live, but we ain't coming over there. It's bad,*" *Tiffany's cousin Tuesday said with an attitude.*

"*We'll be over there. I want my money. What time?*" *Tiffany spoke up and asked.*

"*What?*" *Tuesday asked with her hands on her hips.*

"*Aight, well, I'll see you later, cutie.*" *Mercy walked off.*

Later that night, Tiffany was sucking him up in the dope house he was shacking up at with his mother after he gave her three hundred dollars. He should have known if she was fucking him on the first night in a dope house that she was a hoe. But her head game and sex had him so hypnotized he wasn't even thinking straight. Not to mention he was on a pill and had a little drink.

Jordin shook his head at his thoughts and answered his ringing phone. It was Doll. He lit his blunt and answered the phone …

"Dinner will be ready in two hours, so bring your ass home on time," Doll said through the phone.

He chuckled. "Aight, babe. I'm wrapping shit up. I'll be there."

"You better be."

He hung up the phone and placed his eyes on the door, waiting for Tiffany to come out, hoping she wouldn't be too long …

$$$$$$

Tiffany sat in the waiting room of Planned Parenthood with her shades on, looking around the room. She was hoping she didn't see anyone she knew or somebody that knew her, but she didn't know them. She was a little embarrassed that she was sitting in an abortion clinic that was right in her neighborhood. She thought Jordin was foul for bringing her there, and she was never going to forgive him for it. She was now glad that she was getting rid of the baby, but she was going to make Jordin's life a living hell once she left his shop. She felt like she had played his fool for too many years, and she couldn't believe she allowed it to happen. He had kept her a secret, and she knew if she wanted to be with him, she had to play the role.

As she waited for her name to be called, she put her earbuds in her ear and played the song she had loved for so long. It always reminded her of when she first met Jordin. When she met him, he was broke and young. He was thugging in the streets heavy, and she was right by his side. However, she was with him because he was the only nigga she trusted to get money with.

She started thinking about the night she committed to being his ride or die. She then started thinking about the night he got shot. When she heard the news, she was devastated, but when she went to visit him, his room was always occupied by Doll. She never said anything about them messing around. She just knew he was on his deathbed, and she had to be there just as much as Doll, so when Doll wasn't there taking care of him, she crept in his room and talked to him while he was in a coma. She remembered crying over his bed, and asking God to give him another chance. Now she wished he was dead.

"T. Davis!" a nurse shouted out, snapping her out her thoughts. Tiffany stood up and walked to the back with the nurse.

Tiffany walked to the back, and the nurse had her take off her clothes and put on a gown. She was then asked to give them a urine sample. She went into the bathroom and emptied her bladder. She then walked back into her room and waited on the doctor. A few minutes later, a doctor came in with a woman that was wheeling in a sonogram machine.

"Ms. Davis, you are indeed pregnant, so I'd like to know if you will be keeping your child?" the doctor asked.

"No, I will be terminating today," she said in a bitter tone.

"Okay, my tech here will do a sonogram to see how far along you are, and then we can go from there." The doctor stood up.

The nurse did her sonogram, and within minutes, she was told that she was almost three months and still had time to terminate her pregnancy with the pill. Wanting to get out of there, she agreed to take the pill. She was given the pill on the spot with a prescription for a couple other meds she would need. Tiffany left the clinic brokenhearted, knowing within a couple of hours, she would be in pain from her baby disconnecting from her body. She vowed if she ever got pregnant again, she was keeping her baby regardless.

When Tiffany got back into the car, she was distraught and pissed off. She didn't even get in the car. She didn't want to ride with him and decided to find her own ride. Jordin rolled the window down.

"You ready?" Jordin asked as he started up his car.

"I'm not going anywhere with you! I fucking hate you. You made me kill my baby!" Tiffany tossed the ultrasound pictures that she had stolen from her chart and her proof that she was given the abortion pill. "I hope you're happy, bitch!" She stormed off from his car and across the parking lot. Jordin reached over and picked up the sonogram pictures. He looked at them and felt absolutely nothing. He was glad she went in and got the pregnancy terminated. He tossed her paperwork and sonogram out the window and drove out of the parking lot, headed to Doll with his situation with Tiffany pushed to the back of his mind.

CHAPTER EIGHT

*D*onovan sat in his office, rolling his stress balls in hand as his assistant and his girlfriend, Lisha, ran off at the mouth on how she messed up a business deal yet again. He was so tired of her fuck ups, but he knew he was part of the problem. He had her spoiled, so she sometimes slipped up in business because she was so *dickmitized*. He had met her three years back at a business gathering. She was introduced to him by a collogue of his and said she'd just graduated from college and was looking for an internship, and he gladly took her under his wing. However, late nights in his office turned into love making and her moving into his condo a month later. She was a good employee but a lousy lover, and that always got in the way of business deals. He had to admit he was too but he always felt that she made him that way with her infidelities.

"I'm so sorry, Donni. But they did promise to meet with you personally if you wanted to." She slid the client's card across the desk. Donni sat his stress balls in their case and picked up the card.

"You know how much this deal means to me. Having a gym built in my own city is a good look for me, and you are messing it up because you left some of the details out last minute. I shouldn't have to go back and beg for deals after you were supposed to nail them. What's going on with you?" he asked as he looked her in the eyes over the desk.

She sighed. "I'm pregnant. Four months to be exact. I was sick this morning, so I was late, and I forgot my notes. I'm so sorry."

"So you are going to drop that bombshell on me right now? I thought you were on birth control ..."

"Well, you are a part of the problem too, Donavan. You are the one that fucking knocked me up in the middle of a business deal. I stopped taking those damn things; they were making me sick! I can't do everything for you. I just can't!" Tears started to fall from her face. Her pregnancy had her emotions at an all-time high, and Donni's usual pressure didn't make her feel any better.

Donni sighed. He had other things on his mind, and he didn't have time to comfort her because she was carrying his child. He didn't want to be selfish, but his business was only two years old, and consumers didn't take him seriously, because he was new in the gym franchise game. Donni was a fitness and wellness trainer that owned three gyms in the city of Los Angeles. Everyone that showed up to his gyms was somebody that wanted to train with him and his team.

"Well, you know our relationship has been wishy-washy, so what are you going to do?" Donni raised his eyebrow. The two had a better relationship as business partners than they did a personal relationship. But they liked each other in their own way. Donni was always searching for someone else, while Lisha did her thing with men as well, so the pregnancy was questionable to him.

"What do you mean, *what am I going to do?* I'm going to have my baby, and you are going to help me take care of it!"

"Not until I find out if it's mine. You know what the hell I mean!"

"You know this is your baby! You know what? You wanna play that game; fine with me. We can get that done before the baby comes. We'll be getting a paternal DNA test. Oh, and whatever we had, it's done!" She tossed her work folders on his desk and stormed out. Her work day was over, and she was contemplating on taking off the whole week.

"Yeah, we never had anything to begin with!" His office door slammed.

Donni flopped back down in his office chair and rubbed his temples. Now he had to worry about having a child with Lisha, and he didn't want to. He loved kids, but he never wanted to just have a baby mother. He wanted a family, and he knew all Lisha wanted was money. True, she helped him on the business side, but she got paid for everything she did and even got a little extra.

His office phone began to ring once she stormed out. When he looked to see who was calling, it was his aunt Elsa. He smiled and picked up his phone.

"Yes, Aunty," Donni said through the phone.

"Nephew, I need you to take me over on Compton Ave. to this medical marijuana clinic called Flight Gods. Today," his aunt demanded.

"Okay, but why can't you ask my mother or Stacey? She's not working today. And why are you going to a weed shop?"

"Because I don't want them in my business, and I know your ass smokes weed too. It's a shop that I always see on Instagram, and they have good deals."

"Aunt E, you know you're my favorite, but what are you doing on Instagram? Didn't your doctor say you wasn't supposed to look at your phone screen too long because of your cataracts?"

"Boy, don't worry about my eyes. You just worry about being here in twenty minutes. I'm already ready." She hung up the phone.

Aunt Elsie was so bossy and so hip to everything that was going on in the world. She was popular on social media for her bright clothing she wore and sassy, carefree attitude at the age of sixty-five. She was his mother's oldest sister, and she had his back to the fullest, and he had hers. She had gotten him out of so much trouble that his mother didn't know about, so he wasn't really surprised that she knew about a weed shop in Compton.

Donni looked at the time and saw it was one in the afternoon. He did all his meetings for the day and decided to work on the deal Lisha possibly messed up the next day. He called his receptionist and told her he would be leaving for the day. He loved being his own boss because he could leave anytime he wanted. He packed up his things and walked down to his Bentley truck. He started it up and headed to his aunt's house that was located on the westside of Compton.

$$$$$

Doll walked into the weed shop and saw things were already picking up, and it was only ten in the morning. She had been working there on her off days for a couple hours since Jordin was in between hiring. She liked working in his shops on her off days because it was better than being at home. When she looked to see who was working the counter, Jordin was there, serving a customer. She smiled. Usually,

Jordin was nowhere to be found at eleven in the morning, but he was there, getting work done. She walked over to him and sat her purse down on the glass counter.

"What's up, babe? I'm surprised to see you here at ten in the morning," Doll said as she reached in for a kiss.

"Gotta get up and get this money. That nigga Janario is out of town, so I had to open today. But what's up with you? What you got in that bag?" Jordin asked as he eyed the Norms diner bag she was holding.

"Food for me." She smirked, knowing he wanted to ask if she had gotten him anything. She didn't even know he would be in the shop so early, seeing as he usually showed up after noon for a couple hours and then leave.

"Food for you, huh? I see you, babe," Mercy said as he poured grams of weed from a Mason jar for the customer he was serving.

"I'll see you later." She smirked at him and then walked off and headed to the back of the shop to lock up her purse and eat her food.

Twenty minutes later, Doll started walking toward the front of the shop. But as she was walking, she was stopped by Ariana.

"Hey, Doll. What's, up? I heard Tiffany got fired. How true is that?" Ariana asked.

"What's up, girl? Jordin hasn't told me shit. But it's about time," she said as they walked toward the front slowly so they could continue their conversation.

"Mercy has been here since this morning, checking everybody

about being late and giving out too much weed. Tiffany came in and got her little belongings she had here and told us she wasn't working here anymore. She started calling him all kind of bitch ass niggas. She even called him a cheater. I don't know what that was about." Ariana shrugged.

"Oh, really … Well, I'll find out and let ya know." Doll walked off, and headed to the front. She wasn't surprised that Jordin didn't tell her about Tiffany being fired. He was always so offhand when it came to Tiffany. But the fact that she was calling him a cheater was what really had her mind wondering. But she decided to ask him about it later. She was ready to have a good day, drama free. Especially since Tiffany was no longer there.

Doll knew she had served at least twenty people in the last hour. Money was flowing in, and she could see why Jordin insisted that he take care of her. But she knew none of it was promised if he continued to sell dope. When she looked to see who they had let in, she saw a familiar face walking in with an older woman. Doll was a little uncomfortable seeing him, especially with Jordin in the shop, watching everything that was going on.

"Hello, the beautiful, Doll. I am so glad to meet you, baby girl. The owner of this place posts you all over his Instagram, so I know that face from anywhere. I have been waiting a while to come here and meet you both," Elsa said as she walked up to the counter. Jordin made it his duty that he showed off his wife on their business page and his personal page.

"Thank you for the compliment. Miss—"

"You can just call me Aunty E like my nephew does." She smiled as Donni helped her onto the barstool that was sitting in front of the glass counter.

"And hello, Doll," Donni said, pleased to have run into Doll again. He couldn't lie. After partying with her a few nights ago, he couldn't get her off his mind. When Lisha wasn't around, he thought about seeing her again and what would happen if they did. Now seeing her sober, he got to see her true beauty. She had a beauty mark on her chin, and her pretty brown eyes were to die for.

"Hello, Donni. I see we meet again," Doll said as she reached in the glass counter to pull out jars of weed and her pink scale.

"So you and my nephew know each other, I see," Elsa said with a smile.

"Hardly, E. She is just a girl I met at the club. That's all." He shrugged, not trying to impose too much in front of his aunt.

"I done got all the way here and have to use the bathroom. Pull out your finest strands. I'm buying a gram of it all," Elsa said as she stepped off the stool. Doll told her where the restroom was, and she walked off.

Donni sat on the barstool his aunt was sitting in and leaned in closer to Doll. He was waiting for a moment to talk to her while his aunt wasn't sitting there, so he was taking this time.

"I don't think you should slide close to me, playboy. My husband is right over there serving a customer. Not only is he a budtender, but he is the owner, so I'd advise you to scoot back to where you were," Doll said as she discreetly pointed at Mercy.

"Well, let me just give you my card. Call me sometimes. I know you are married, but I know you can have friends." He smiled as he slid his card from the inside of his phone case wallet. He then tossed it on the counter.

"You're really fucking bold. I don't think I will be calling you, Donni." She slid his card to the side.

At that moment, Jordin looked over and saw that Donni had moved closer to Doll. He had been watching them the whole time, making sure dude did not get close to his woman. Doll saw the expression on his face as he walked away from the customer he was serving and walked off toward Doll. Donni saw him coming, but he did not move away from Doll. For some reason, he was feeling bold. He could tell just by the look on Mercy's face that he wasn't the average business owner. His face looked like he had been through some things in his past with the mean mug he wore and the way he gripped at his waistline, letting them know he was securing his gun. At the same time Mercy approached, so did Elsa. She sat down. and Doll started opening jars of weed.

"What's up, homie? Don't you think you are a little too close to my budtender?" Mercy asked as he stood over Donni with a mean mug on his face.

Donni looked over at Doll, and Doll was already tending to Elsa. She was not jumping to anything. Donni was a cool guy, but Jordin was her husband, and she knew not to take up for Donni, no matter how mad she was at him. Her loyalty was with Jordin.

Donni stood up. "My bad, *homie?* You the manager or something? I didn't think there was a rule on how close I could be to your budtender.

But I'll move back." Donni threw his hands up and backed away. He wasn't scared. He was actually being sarcastic.

Nigga, got a gun in his waist. Probably can't knock nobody out, though, Donni said to himself as he continued to smirk at the print of Jordin's gun seeping through his shirt.

Mercy noticed all the smirking he was doing, and he wasn't feeling it. "Nah, I'm the owner, fam. You see something funny around here?" Mercy asked as he continued to frown.

"Babe, please. I have a customer sitting here, and she is elderly. Can you just step outside, sir, until I finish serving your aunt?" she begged slightly. She knew Jordin had a temper, and she didn't want Donni taking him out of his element in front of customers.

"Is there a problem here, young man? This is my nephew, and he is just here to assist me," Elsa said as she turned around and looked at Mercy. She could feel the tension between Mercy and Donni, and she didn't know why.

"There's no problem here, ma'am. He was just sitting too close to my wife, and I don't appreciate that," he stated boldly.

"Jordin, don't start. Just go back to helping customers. He's leaving." Doll looked at Donni and gave him a look she hoped he understood.

"Yeah, I'm leaving. Just help my aunt outside when she's done." Donni walked off with Mercy burning a hole in his back, watching him leave the shop. He then looked at Doll, and she shrugged her shoulders.

"I want to talk to you in my office when you are done," Mercy said and walked off.

"Sheesh, Miss lady. You got men swarming over you. Don't let them be your downfall, though. Overprotective men always seem to be a woman's downfall," Elsa said as though she knew Doll's life.

At times, she did feel like she would fail with Mercy in her life, doing illegal things and having a bad attitude when customers were around. She didn't know if he were being watched by the police or watched by his haters on the streets. She knew if police came and took Mercy away, they would lose everything fighting his case. Or if he died, nothing would ever be the same for her, so Elsa was right.

"I know. I'm focused on my job outside working here. I'm a lab tech, and these men will never be my downfall. But here is everything you asked for. I threw in a few edibles and pre-rolled joints," Doll said as she handed Elsa her pharmacy bag filled with all her THC goodies.

Elsa looked in the bag and smiled. "Thank you so much, and I will be back when all of this is gone." Elsa pulled out her debit card and handed it to Doll.

After Elsa paid, she handed Doll a hefty tip in cash, and Doll helped her to the car. When she helped her in, Donni didn't say a word. He helped his aunt with her seatbelt and drove off.

Doll sighed and walked back into the shop. She didn't want to go to Mercy's office, because she knew the argument was Donni. She was glad he didn't notice that it was the guy from the club that she was dancing with. But now that he had gotten a good look at Donni, he wasn't going to forget his face.

Mercy never forgot a face ...

Doll walked down the hall, listening to heels click on the marble floor that led to the back of the shop to Mercy's office. She could hear music playing. She knew he was probably in his office, pacing and trying to find his words. However, Doll had a comeback for anything he threw at her. He was still in the hot seat, and she was also holding onto information about Tiffany.

When she opened his door, just as she expected, he was pacing his floor with weed smoke coming out his nose like a bull. He stopped pacing when she walked in. He looked at his beautiful wife and his temper came down just a notch. She was bad, and he knew men were going to try their hand even if he were around. But he knew if he didn't get his shit together, Doll might leave him for one of those men that wanted to take his place.

"What's up, Jordin? We have customers, and you're having a tantrum. What's with you?" Doll asked as she closed the door and walked toward him.

"So you just let niggas be all in your space now? This is the second time, Doll. What the fuck," Jordin said in a frustrated tone. He walked over to his desk and dumped his ashes in his ashtray.

"Nigga, in my space? He wasn't even that close to me. You need to stop paying so much attention to me when a guy is talking to me. The music was loud, and he asked me a question. That was all," Doll lied.

"Yeah, if you say so. I don't like seeing other niggas close to you. You're going to fuck around and get one of these niggas killed."

"You're tripping, and you need to control your temper ..." Doll flopped on his couch.

"My temper is fine. You just need to stop being so friendly." He sat behind his desk.

"Look who's talking … So you fired Tiffany, huh?" Doll asked with a smirk on her face as she gradually put the spotlight on him.

"Yeah, I did … Who told you that?" Jordin asked as he looked at Doll. He was watching her body language and face to see if she was mad or knew anything more.

"Somebody that works here … Why did you fire her all of a sudden?"

"Because I know you don't want her here, so I finally let her go. I have ninety days to get right, right?"

"You sure do, and I don't know what Tiffany has to do with that. But I also heard that she called you a cheater, so if I find out you've been fuckin' with that bitch or any other bitch, this marriage is over, and I'm filing for divorce; fuck a separation."

Doll could feel herself getting angry. One thing she didn't like was being a fool for a man. She had trusted Jordin with her heart and married him on a drop of a dime, so it would be so hurtful if he had committed the ultimate sin.

"Yeah, I hear you, babe. I'll be out front in a little bit." Jordin sat at his desk and went into deep thought. Every time the thought of Doll leaving him crossed his mind, he got weak to the knees. He knew he wasn't shit for lying to his wife. But now that he had Tiffany out of his life, he was ready to move forward.

"Well, I'm leaving. I'm not even in the mood to help you. I'm going to meet up with Breann until later." Doll stormed out his office. Her mind began to wander. She was so close to calling Tiffany herself to get answers. She hated the way he brushed her off when it came to her. She was going to Breann and getting some advice of what she should do.

When she walked back up front to leave, Alaina stopped her and handed her a card. "I seen that fine ass nigga all in your grill. You better call him, girl. That nigga Mercy can be replaced." She winked and walked off.

Doll looked at the card. She knew Alaina was right, but she didn't want to start a relationship while she was still married. She truly wanted to work things out with Jordin. But if getting attention from other men was going to be his wakeup call, she was going to use it to her advantage. She stuffed his card in her purse and headed out.

CHAPTER NINE

It's Over...

Two nights Later...

*D*oll lay in her bed with her eyes wide open in the dark as Jordin's phone continued to vibrate on his nightstand. She was annoyed, and he was sleeping right through it. His phone had been going off all day, and she wanted to see who it was he was ignoring. Doll reached on his side of the bed and grabbed his phone. She used his code that she had remembered a while back to open his phone. When she went to the text messages, he had twenty-five unread messages from Tiffany. Doll opened the thread and immediately became mortified at the things she read.

Tiffany Hoe Ass: You see your dead baby in the toilet, bitch. I hope your wife finds out you made me get an abortion, you scum ass, crab ass, nigga!!!

Tiffany Hoe Ass: Tell that bitch Dollaysia about the STD I gave you. That's why you don't fuck her no more!

Tiffany Hoe Ass: I hope our dead baby haunts you in your nightmares, bitch!!!!!

Tiffany Hoe Ass: I wasted seven years of my life on you. That's why I fucked all your homeboys, and they loved this pussy!

Doll could feel her temper flaring as she continued to read the messages as they came in. She dropped Jordin's phone on the bed and punched him in the chest so hard that he woke up gasping for air in the dark.

"Muthafucka, you been cheating on me with Tiffany's dirty ass, and she gave you a STD! That's why you wasn't fucking me, you bum ass nigga?" Doll shouted as she got out of bed and turned on the light. Jordin stood out of bed, still holding his chest. He didn't think a little woman like Doll would get the strength to cave his chest in.

"What the fuck are you talking about, babe?" Jordin asked in a curious tone as he walked toward her.

Doll reached into her nightstand and pulled out the small .22 gun that Jordin kept in there for her. She took the gun and pointed it at Jordin. She had so much hate in her heart that she could blow his head off. He had betrayed her in the worst way. As of recently, she started getting suspicions that he was cheating, but she wanted to be wrong. She wanted money and drugs to be the reason he wasn't coming home. But it was another woman.

"Dollaysia, please put the gun down. Who told you that?" He threw his hands up and stood in his tracks.

"The bitch is in your phone telling you how much she hates you and you made her get an abortion. You've been with this bitch for seven years, and you married me four years ago? You took me out my comfort zone to treat me like shit!" Doll cried out. Tears fell from her eyes. She was heartbroken and angry. She felt used and disgusted. She and Jordin had never tried to conceive a baby, and here Tiffany was, saying she had an abortion.

"I'm sorry, babe. I should have told you, but I wanted you. I didn't want her. Our business relationship turned into something personal, and I didn't want it to go that way," he pleaded.

"That's bullshit, Jordin! I'm packing my shit, and I'm leaving. I don't want you to touch me or contact me. I'm getting a lawyer. And if you try and stop me, I swear I'll fucking kill you!"

Jordin backed away. He knew a heartbroken woman when he saw one, and he knew not to get in the way. He walked over to the bed and started rubbing his temples while Doll went into their closet and tore it up, packing her belongings. Jordin was finally exposed, and it hurt him to the core knowing he hurt Doll. He led her on to think he was a good man, and he was anything but. Jordin picked up his phone and saw all the messages Doll had read. He saw the picture of the fetus she had passed in her toilet, and that made him livid.

"Doll knows I was fucking with your hoe ass, and now she is leaving me. I hope you are happy, you slut. But I still ain't fucking with you, and you better hope I don't kill your ass. You will never be Dollaysia!" Jordin texted back to her with a middle finger emoji.

Doll walked out of the closet and rolled her bag toward the door. Jordin looked at her with sad eyes. She was still holding her gun in her hand, making sure he didn't stop her from leaving.

"I'm sorry we have to end like this, babe. I hope we can work shit out. I've been changing, and I'm going to continue to try and do better."

"Yeah, you do that ..." Doll said as she walked out the door.

When she got behind her wheel, she broke down and cried in agony. She was so crushed, and she was embarrassed. She knew everyone in his shop had to know about him and Tiffany. She felt like she had to be the only one that didn't know. That was how embarrassed and low she felt. She was paranoid, thinking that the whole world knew she was getting cheated on.

After crying her eyes out in her driveway, she dried her eyes and started her truck. She decided to drive to Breann's and tell her the news. She didn't want to go to a hotel, because she didn't want to drown in her misery alone. She knew Breann would be there for her, so she hopped on the freeway and headed to Compton ...

$$\$\$\$\$\$$$

Breann rode Janario's dick slowly as Aaliyah's song "One in a Million" played in the background lowly. The twins were gone with her mother for a few days, so they were taking advantage with some love making. Janario smacked her ass hard and then gripped it. He started stroking her slowly from the bottom while he nibbled on her neck.

"Mmmm, Janario, I love you." Breann moaned as he pounded her pussy.

"I love you too, bae," Janario seductively said back. He loved Breann, and no other female compared to her. He watched his boys go from female to female, and he even watched Jordin cheat on his wife. Meanwhile, he stayed with his down ass female and had no plans on leaving her.

At that moment, they heard their doorbell ringing. Janario stopped stroking her, and they looked at each other.

"Go see who that is and come right back," Breann said.

"Nah, let me get my nut first. I'm about to bust anyway," Janario said as he started stroking her.

Breann laughed and then shook her head. She began riding him like her life depended on it. After riding him for a few more minutes, Janario burst inside of her. The doorbell was still ringing, so Breann got off him and grabbed her robe.

"I'm about to curse whoever this is out," Breann said as she slipped on her slippers.

Janario slipped on his basketball shorts and walked over to their bedroom window. He could see who was standing at their gate. He shook his head when he saw Doll rolling her luggage through the gate.

"This nigga Mercy done got caught up. Stupid," Janario said to himself as he walked over to the dresser and grabbed his phone. He had five missed calls from Jordin.

He sat on the bed and returned his call.

"Nigga, what happened?" Janario asked as soon as Jordin answered the phone.

"Dollaysia left a nigga. Tiffany kept texting my phone, and she read the texts. That bitch Tiffany was saying all kind of shit. I'ma pop that bitch." Jordin started coughing. He was smoking.

"Damn, nigga. I told your dumb ass to leave that bitch alone. We could have got another bitch to drive across state. But you had to have her." Janario shook his head.

"I fucked up, bro."

"Yeah, you did, nigga. But I'ma drive up there since your girl's here. That's the only way I'm a get some sleep because they are going to be up talking about your hoe ass all night." Janario stood up and slipped on his Nikes and shirt.

Jordin chuckled. "Aight, bro."

Janario packed up his duffle bag and headed downstairs. When he made it to the living room, he spotted Doll and Breann sitting on the couch. Doll was crying while Breann wore a mean mug on her face while she held Doll's hand in hers. He knew shit was about to get crazy, and he didn't want Breann all in the mix. But he knew now that Jordin's secret was out, she was going to be there for her friend.

"I'm about to step out for a minute, Bre," Janario said as he walked up to Breann and kissed her on the forehead.

"You're going by that dog ass nigga Mercy's?" Breann asked with an attitude.

"Yeah ... I'm a go talk some sense into this nigga." He grabbed his car keys from the coffee table.

"Yeah, please do that, because he is a fucked-up individual," Doll said as she wiped her nose and eyes with a tissue.

"Don't trip. I got y'all. But I'm a see you tomorrow, babe." Janario kissed her again and headed out the door.

When Janario walked out the door, Breann sighed. She felt so bad for Doll and wished she could have saved her a heartache a long time ago. She knew Jordin was cheating, and she was so glad it finally came out to the light.

"I can't believe he's had been lying to me all this time. I wish I would have gotten screenshots. She said she just had an abortion a couple days ago, and she gave him an STD. She sent him the pictures of the damn baby in the toilet. I'm going to have to go get tested for HIV now."

"I'm so sorry this is going on. And I'm so sorry I couldn't tell you," Breann confessed.

"What do you mean, you are sorry *you couldn't tell me?*" Doll asked.

"I knew Jordin and Tiffany were fucking around, but Janario didn't want me in y'all business. She was their runner, but I know for a fact her and Jordin were fuckin'."

Doll took her hands away from Breann. "You mean to tell me you knew all this time?"

"Yes, and I'm sorry. I didn't want anything to happen to me or my kids. Janario knows Jordin has a temper. Had I told you what was going on, he would kill me," Breann said sincerely.

Doll stood up. "You mean to tell me you had me walking around here looking stupid? I can't believe you. We are supposed to be best friends!"

"Doll, I told you when you first told me you made it official with him, but you didn't want to hear me. I told you from the beginning what the nigga was going to do to you. I'm sorry, but I just couldn't tell you." Breann began to cry.

"I can't believe this shit. I need some time alone. I will just find me a damn hotel. Everyone is stabbing me in the back," Doll said in disgust as she walked toward the door. She was pissed off at Breann, and she needed time away from her. She was so hurt and felt like everyone was being selfish and inconsiderate of her feelings.

Breann stood up and called out to Doll. "Dollaysia, wait. You have to understand!"

"Fuck you, Bre. I'm out." Doll stormed out with her luggage and headed to her truck.

She was done with Breann and their friendship …

CHAPTER TEN

Moving Along

One week later...

$\mathcal{D}$oll watched her mother drop three sugar cubes in her tea and stir it lightly as the hot steam blew in her face. It was eight in the morning, and they had just come from a mile run. She looked over at her mother as she stirred her tea. Her mother was so bourgeoisie and only used fine china and silver spoons for her tea. But she admired her to the fullest. Doll wasn't a girly girl until she met Jordin. All her life, her mother tried to get her to wear dresses and heels, but all she preferred were Polo shirts and jeans. Her mother taught her style and how to be a lady, so when Jordin said he liked his woman in heels and dresses, she knew how to put it together well.

"What's going on with you, Dollaysia? You've been going running with me every morning and staying overnight when you get off work like you don't have a man at home." Her mother, Daria, sipped her tea.

Doll sighed. "I'm only telling you this because you're the only person I trust these days. Jordin was cheating on me the whole time we were together, and everyone knew, except me. Even Breann."

Daria shook her head. "I'm so sorry to hear that. So what are you going to do now? You're still working, right?" her mother asked with concern.

"I'm filing for divorce, and I am going to get my own place. Thank God that I'm still working, and I have so much money in my account. I'll have my place by the end of the week."

"That's my girl. If you need a lawyer, let me know. But you know, your daddy cheated on me, and I didn't leave him …"

Doll raised her eyebrow. "Daddy cheated on you?"

"Yes, Daddy cheated on me, but I know how to keep my business to myself, even from you. He had an affair when I was pregnant with you. But seeing your little face made him turn his life around. We've been together ever since."

"Wow, so you didn't beat his ass or anything?"

Daria laughed. "Oh, yes, we fought, we argued, and we cried. And I always kept faith in him. I loved your father, and I knew he loved me, so I stuck it out."

"Damn. Well, I'm not sticking this one out, tho'. The things I know that he did with that woman, I can't stand to look at him." She shook her head.

"Well, do what you gotta do. You got enough money to buy you a man. I know that hospital is breaking you off."

Doll laughed. "Yeah right. I'm not tricking. But there is this one trainer guy that's crushing on me. He's really cute. We've encountered each other twice already. I've turned him down twice, and he keeps trying. The last time I saw him, he came to Jordin's shop when I was working there. He was bold enough to give me his card to call him while Jordin was watching. Jordin almost killed him already."

"Well, if he's a nice guy, give him a call. No harm in stepping out your marriage if it's already dead. I told you when I first met Jordin I knew he was crazy." Her mother shrugged. She and Doll always talked like they were best friends.

"I'm going to do that just because I can." Doll laughed and then stood up. She headed to her old room to shower and get ready for the day.

When she walked into her room, she sat on the bed and pulled out her wallet to look for her lawyer's number. As she was going through her business cards, she ran across Donni's card. It had a picture of him on his card, flexing his muscles, with a huge smile on his face. She laughed to herself at his cheesy smile. He had his cell number on the card and his office number. She decided to send him a text.

"Hey, its Doll. Thought I'd slide you a text." She hit send. Before she could put her phone down, a text came through.

"Thanks for sliding me a text, beautiful. Let's meet up at my gym later. I'd love to see you."

She smiled … *"Let's do that. Tell me a time, and I'll be there."*

"6:30… let's have a vegan dinner, on me."

"I'd like that."

Doll sat on the bed and went into deep thought. She knew she could live life without a man in her life, but she felt like her career was on track, and she was almost thirty, so looking for a companion wasn't doing her any harm. Jordin had fucked up, but she wasn't closing her heart because he had fucked up his chance with her. She felt like she deserved real love, so she was giving someone else a chance to love her.

It was still early in the day, so she decided to go out looking for an apartment. She felt like she was getting a fresh start at life. She was free and didn't have to worry about Jordin breathing over her shoulder because he was the one doing wrong. Therefore, she was going to do what she wanted, and she was starting with meeting with Donni …

$$$$$

Later that Evening …

Donni lay back on the bench, getting ready to bench press two hundred pounds. He adjusted his gloves, and then he looked up at his best friend, Jap, who was spotting for him.

"You ready?" Jap asked with a grin on his face.

"Yup." Donni gripped the bar and proceeded to lift the two-hundred-pound weights. Lifting two hundred pounds of metal felt like he was lifting a horse. But he had the strength, and he was energized enough to push through.

"One … Two … Three …" Jap counted, making sure his friend didn't skip a beat.

Donni couldn't take it anymore after ten presses. He sat the bar in its place and sat up.

"Arrggg, I feel great! I'm ready for my date now." Donni stood up and stretched.

"I can't believe ol' girl is finally giving you a chance. She must be leaving her husband or some shit," Jap said as he sat on the weight bench and sipped his Gatorade.

"I don't know, but she surprised the hell out of me when she texted me. I thought I was going to never hear from her again the way her husband was trippin." Donni shrugged and wiped sweat from his head.

"Well, you know ya girl gonna be jealous when she sees you fuckin' with somebody else."

"Well, she can keep being jealous. She said she's keeping the baby, so I guess that's something I do have to worry about."

Jap shook his head. "Trappin' you, damn."

"Yeah, trappin' a nigga. But I'm going to get at you later. She should be here soon," Donni said as he looked at his iWatch.

The two slapped fives, and Donni headed to his private shower room. After he showered, he headed inside his office and threw on a pair of sweats and a tank top. He slid his diamonds in his ears and slid on his rope chain. He then got on his phone and ordered a feast of his favorite vegan dishes. He then called up his front-desk assistant to let her know when Doll came. Forty-five minutes later, his food and Doll showed up at the same time.

"What's up, beautiful? Have a seat," Donni said as he set the food on the table.

"Whatever you have in those bags smells good. I love vegan food," Doll said as she slid out of her sweater and sat down. She was wearing a pair of Nike leggings and a matching sports bra.

"I'm glad you love it because I do too. I'm vegan five times out of the week."

"That's cool. I have an okay diet, but it could be better. I thought I'd do some working out before I go. Your gym is nice."

"Thanks, I worked hard to get this place just right. Now I'm working on a few more franchises."

"That's wassup. I like that you are a boss."

"Oh yeah? So what made you text me? You were shy when we last saw each other; now you're sitting in my office like that never happened."

"A lot has happened since we last seen each other, Donni," she sighed. She contemplated on not telling him what was going on in her life. She didn't want to appear as weak. But she wanted him to be aware of what was going on with her. "I'm getting a divorce ..."

"Damn, that's deep ... May I ask why?" Donni started taking their food out the bags.

"He crossed the line too many times in our marriage, so I think it's best we both work on our careers and go our separate ways."

"That's fair. Well, I'm glad you called me. You must want me to be your rebound nigga or something," he chuckled.

"No, I just thought you were a cool guy. I wanted to get to know. You're the first guy I've let in my space in four years."

"I'm flattered ... So since you want to get to know me, and you seem like you need a getaway—going through a divorce and all—I was thinking we get away for a day or two to get to know each other. I'm visioning breakfast in Paris and a little sightseeing before we leave. We can leave in a couple hours on my jet if you want," Donni said casually like Paris was right around the corner.

Doll laughed as she piled her plate with spaghetti squash. "I'm envisioning you're a damn fool if you think I'm going to Paris with you."

"What's wrong? You're scared or you don't have a passport?"

"I have a passport, and no, I'm not scared. I'm just not flying anywhere with anyone I just met."

"That's fine, but I'm going anyway, so if you change your mind, give me a call," Donni said in a bitter tone.

"Let's not let that spoil the night. Let's finish this food, and you can go train me for an hour," she smiled.

"Alright, that's cool. But I'm not going to be easy on you." He winked.

"Trust me. I can handle anything."

As they ate their food, Doll thought Donni must have been rolling in dough to just up and go to Paris on such short notice. But as impressed as she was, she wasn't going to let him talk her out of her panties. She just needed a little company to get Jordin off her mind and possibly get to know Donni, not make him her man overnight.

As they were finishing up their meal, there was a knock at the door. Before Donni could tell them to come in, the door flew open. It was Lisha, and she didn't look happy. She walked in and eyed Doll as she walked toward his desk.

"What's up, Lisha? I'm having dinner. What did I tell you about barging in?" Donni stood up from his desk.

"I don't mean to barge in on you and your new little *girlfriend*. But I wanted to let you know that I'm stepping down from my position as being your assistant. I found a new job and a new man. I won't need you anymore, and you are now free to do what the fuck you want. Have fun with him, sis, because eventually, you'll be pregnant, taking a fucking DNA test on your unborn child." Lisha slapped a folder in front of him and stormed out his office.

"Damn, that was awkward," Doll said as she shook her head.

"I'm sorry about that. Some people just don't know how to be professional." He opened the folder, and there was a piece of paper in it that said Lisha's baby was his. Part of him wanted the baby to be someone else's, but he knew now he had to step up and be a man.

"So who is she, Donni? Don't start with the secrets. That's why me and my husband are divorcing, so lay it all out on the table before the leading on starts." Doll crossed her arms.

"She's my now ex-girlfriend, and she is carrying my child … That's what's on this paper. We got a noninvasive DNA test." He slid the folder to her.

"Wow …" Doll shook her head as she read over the results. She knew he was too good to be true. She knew he had a flaw sitting somewhere. He had a baby's mother …

"I will understand if you don't want to kick it with me anymore. But if you are willing to continue to get to know me, I promise my baggage won't even be in your face."

He's honest, Doll thought to herself. Getting the truth out of Jordin was like pulling a wisdom tooth, but Donni had balls. He had no reason to hide anything going on in his life.

"You have a child on the way; that's always going to be in my face if I decide to ever be with you."

"You're right. That's why I'm leaving it all up to you if you ever want to be with me."

"Alright, Donavan. We'll see." She stood up from his desk, and he did as well.

They left the conversation at that and headed out to the gym area for a workout.

CHAPTER ELEVEN

Dirty...

"*S*tupid ass bitch!"

Jordin took his fist and rammed it into Tiffany's face for the second time. He had barged into her house at one in the morning while she was sleeping to let off some steam. He was angry, and he was high off two pills. The pills had his mind gone and temper flaring. Now he was taking it all out on Tiffany. His heart was broken, and he thought he was going crazy. Doll had left him, and she wasn't answering any of his calls. After he got their divorce papers in the mail, that was when he realized their breakup was real. He blamed Tiffany for everything, even knowing all of it was his fault. He knew he had used Tiffany, and he had used Doll for his own selfish ways. Money and pussy got in the way of him loving his wife the way he was supposed to, and now it had backfired.

"Mercy, please stop hitting me. You're going to make me black out!" Tiffany cried out with blood leaking from her mouth.

Jordin grabbed her by the throat while he lay on top of her. He looked her into the eyes as he snarled at her. She knew he wasn't in his right mind, and she was scared to death. Jordin stood up and then picked her up by the throat. Tiffany stood to her feet.

"You like hoeing and being a loud-mouth hoodrat bitch, so I'ma treat you like one." Jordin threw her on the couch aggressively. He didn't care how much pain she was in.

Jordin dropped his jeans and pulled out his dick. He was rock hard from the drugs and liquor in his system, and he was ready to release.

"Get on your knees and suck my sick," Jordin demanded.

Jordin had punched her in the jaw when he first walked in, and she was in pain. However, she knew if she wanted to make it out alive, she had to do what he said even if it hurt.

She took him into her mouth halfway, but Jordin grabbed her ponytail and forced his dick down her throat. Tiffany gagged, almost throwing up her last meal. Jordin continued to force feed his dick to her.

"You like that shit, huh, you nasty bitch? This the shit my homies like, huh?" Jordin asked in a seductive yet demonic tone as he looked down at her gagging for dear life.

Jordin finally let her come up for air. She quickly caught her breath. Jordin looked down at her and laughed. She looked a mess, and she looked defeated. "You talked a lot of shit about me to everybody and even in my texts. My wife saw that shit. You knew it was over between us, and you still wanted to latch on to some shit that was never there."

"Mercy, it's not my fault your wife found you out. You got caught up; I didn't get you caught up!" she cried out.

"I don't give a fuck, bitch. When I said leave me alone, you should have done that shit." He shoved his dick back in her mouth, this time causing her to vomit. He slapped her across the face so hard she started seeing flashing lights.

"Look what you did, bitch! Go get a towel and clean my dick off," Jordin demanded.

Tiffany stood to her feet and walked to the bathroom. Her head was spinning, and she knew he had to get out of Jordin's presence. When she walked into the bathroom, she looked at her face. Her nose was leaking, her lip was busted, and her hair was a mess. Jordin had beat her in the worst way, and she knew she wasn't going to see daylight anytime soon. No matter how much he had beat her, she knew she couldn't call the police on him. She knew if she got him locked up, shit would get uglier for her. She turned on the sink and rinsed some of the blood from her face.

"Hurry the fuck up! My dick's getting soft. You think I wanna be here all night with throw up on my dick?" Jordin shouted through the door.

Tiffany walked out the bathroom with a warm rag for his dick and one to clean the floor. After she cleaned the floor, she wiped his dick, and Mercy shoved it back into her mouth.

"Oh shit, I'm about to cum." Jordin took his dick out her mouth and started stroking it.

Tiffany couldn't take being on her knees any longer, so she fell to the floor on her back. Jordin stood over her and let his seeds drop all over her body. After he released, he bent down and slapped her thigh so hard her skin immediately turned red.

"Get up. Let's take a shower." Jordin walked off and headed into the bathroom. Tiffany stood to her feet. Her body was weak, and she felt like she wanted to die. Jordin was making her feel worthless, and she hated that feeling.

When Tiffany walked into the bathroom, Jordin was already in the shower. She sat on the toilet to empty her bladder; then she stepped in with him. As soon as she stepped in, he grabbed her and threw her against the wall.

"Bitch, I'm not done with you. You know what these pills do to me. By the time I'm done with you, you won't have any walls."

Jordin stroked his dick and then shoved it inside of her, missing her pussy and going straight into her ass. Tiffany shouted. She hated anal, and to get it without warning sent her into excruciating pain. Jordin put his hand around her throat and applied pressure as he stroked her roughly. Tiffany was gasping for air, but Jordin was trying to catch his nut.

"Jordin, I can't breathe. Please stop," Tiffany managed to say. But that only caused him to grip her throat tighter. The sound of him pounding her in the hot water had him so horny. As much as he hated Tiffany, her pussy was always good. And for some reason, it was better than ever at that moment.

Jordin felt himself about to cum, but Tiffany's body went limp. Her body began to slip out his hands. He pulled out, and Tiffany slid to the tub floor. Yet again, Jordin let out his load all over her, but this time, over her dead body. He had choked her to death, and he didn't feel sorry for her. Jordin turned around and let the hot water fall over his body while Tiffany lay behind him dead. He washed his body and stepped out like Tiffany wasn't there. He dried off and slipped back on his clothes. He then left Tiffany's house and headed home, feeling like he had gotten his revenge. He got into his brand-new Benz truck and did ninety on the freeway back to his empty home.

$$$$$$

Doll lay in her bed wide awake. She had so many thoughts, and she wished she could escape them. She hated when night came because Jordin haunted her thoughts. She couldn't lie. She still loved him, but she knew she couldn't take him back. He had hurt her in the worst way, so he had to suffer. Donni's offer to Paris wasn't sounding like a bad idea. She was bored, and she needed a change in scenery. She knew Jordin had the divorce papers by now because he was blowing up her phone. She couldn't wait until he signed them so she could live even more.

Doll got out of bed and headed downstairs of her mother's home. She decided to eat a snack and drink some milk so she could fall asleep. As she was walking by the living room, she saw her father knocked out in his recliner, and her mother was laid out on the couch in her robe. She had the remote in her hand, flipping through channels. Doll went into the kitchen, poured a glass of milk, and then walked into the living room.

"What's up, Doll? What you are doing up?" Daria asked as she sat up.

"I can't seem to sleep. I have so much on my mind." Doll sighed and then sipped her milk.

"Jordin still haunting your mental?" her mother asked.

"Yes, and he has been calling me non-stop tonight. I was thinking about meeting with him, but I don't know." She shrugged.

"I think you should let him plead his case at least before the divorce. What happened with the trainer guy you were telling me about?"

"I met with him tonight, but first, I want to ask you something. The trainer guy, his name is Donavan. He invited me to fly to Paris with him tonight, but I declined. I mean, I just hooked up with him. I can't fly to Paris."

"You turned down Paris?" her mother asked with a laugh.

"Yes, I can't just leave with him. Why? You think I should have went?" Doll asked out of curiosity.

Daria stood to her feet. "Let's go into the office so you can tell me everything you know about this Donavan."

They both headed upstairs and headed into the home office. Daria sat behind the desk and turned on the computer. Doll sat in front of the desk. Daria was a retired officer and still had access to police records and many other platforms. She was going to find out who Donavan was so her daughter could make her next move.

"His name is Donavan Bradley, and he owns his own gym in Westwood. He told me his birthday was November second, but didn't give me a year. I believe he's thirty-two." Doll left out the fact that he had a baby on the way since he was honest with her. She felt like that situation was personal and something she could handle on her own if she had to.

Daria typed in the information her daughter gave her, and his name and faced popped up. Doll came around the desk with her chair so she could see everything. She loved that her mother had access to personal records. She wished she had done a check on Jordin, but by the time she told her parents about her relationship, she was already three months into her marriage.

"He's handsome …" Daria said as she looked at his DMV picture.

"Yes, he is. And his smile is amazing." Doll blushed.

"He's six feet three, thirty-one years old, lives in Westwood, not married, self-employed, no criminal history, never been locked up at all. Only thing he has is a couple speeding tickets for driving fast in his Bentley. Looks like somebody needs to dust off their passport," Daria smiled.

"So you think I should go? You think I should just leave?" Doll was nervous now that she was getting her mother's approval.

"You're about to be twenty-nine years old and going through your first divorce. Go live your life. How many women get invited to Paris by a fine ass, black, rich man. Because the brother is paid. I hacked his Credit Karma just now. Look at his credit." Daria was good with computers and could hack into anything.

"Mom! Close that. I'm not going with him for his money; I'm going with him because I have a genuine interest in him. Jordin had money; he did everything for me. Now I'm looking to be independent and in control of my relationships."

"I hear you, Doll. Well, tell me how Paris is. I can't get your lazy ass daddy to go anywhere anymore. I remember when you first got your passport. We all went to Jamaica."

Doll stood up and laughed. "Daddy's old now. He's not getting out that recliner for anything. And Jamaica was so fun. I guess I need to go see if the offer stands then. I'll let you know if I'm leaving tonight."

"Okay, baby girl. Have fun, and leave his number in my phone so I can call you if I feel like something is wrong."

Doll laughed. "Okay, Mom. You hacked his life, so I'm sure if something goes wrong, you will find him."

"I sure will. Your daddy was upset when you ran off and married Jordin. Broke his heart. So this man better do right."

"Daddy was mad?" Doll stood up. She and her father never talked too much about her marrying Jordin. She and her dad were close, but she felt the distance once she told him she was married, but he never said he was upset.

"Yes, he thinks Jordin is a scum, so when you tell him you are getting a divorce, lay it on him easy. That's something he would get out his recliner for." Daria stood up.

"Damn … well, don't tell him, Mom. I'll let the ink dry on my divorce papers before I tell him."

"Yeah, you do that."

Doll walked into her room and closed the door. She sat on her bed and gazed at Donni's number. She knew once she asked if the offer still stood, she was opening a new door for love. She hadn't even closed the last one good enough, but she was over Jordin. She wasn't letting their divorce get in the way of something that could potentially be something good—something she knew she should have had from the beginning. *Love...*

Before she pressed call, her phone started vibrating in her hand. It was Jordin, calling for the hundredth time. She sighed. She figured it was time to answer him and see what he wanted. She knew he had to be calling about the divorce papers she had sent to him, so she answered.

"Yes, Jordin," Doll said in a calm tone.

"Why the fuck you haven't been answering my calls, Dollaysia!"

"You know why I haven't been answering your calls. I'm not ready to talk right now. I'm going out of town, so I'll call you in a few days so we can meet and talk." She knew Jordin was fuming on the other end of the phone.

"Stop fuckin' playing with me, Dollaysia. I'm not signing those punk ass divorce papers. You can't leave me. You married me for better or for worse, and you are breaking your vows!" he shouted through the phone. Doll could tell he was drunk.

"You should have thought about your vows before you led me on to think you were a good fucking man, Jordin. Don't call my phone with that vow shit. I said I'll meet with you when I come back. If you can't take that, then I don't know what to tell you." Doll was becoming angry.

"You pulled a fucking gun on me like I'm some fuck nigga. I should have fucked you up! If I don't see you in three days, I'm going to fucking find you, Doll. I'll come up to your job and get you fired. That's all you care about anyway is your punk ass degree."

"Bye, Jordin. You're pissing me off." Doll hung up in his face. She was over arguing with Jordin, and she knew she was going to have to take someone with her to meet with him when the time came. She knew his temper could get out of hand, and she didn't want him hurting her.

Doll put her thoughts of Jordin to the side and proceeded to call Donni. Now she really wanted to leave. She had two days off work, and she was going to call her supervisor and beg for one more day off even though she was on probation.

"Hey, Donavan. It's me ..." Doll said when Donni answered the phone.

"Hey, what's up? You good?" Donni asked, sounding as like he had been sleeping.

"Yeah, I'm good. I was just calling to see if the offer still stands on going to Paris." She smiled as her hands trembled.

"Yea-yeah, it still stands. My jet leaves in the morning, about six. I can have someone come pick you up. How long can you stay?"

"I can only stay two days, maybe three ..."

"Okay, that's all the time I need."

"Okay. Well, I guess I'll see you in the morning." Doll hung up her phone and started packing her things. She was happy, and she was even more happy knowing Jordin was broken and drowning in his own misery. She loved that he had to wait three days while she ran off to Paris with another man.

Doll zipped up her luggage and sat it next to the door. She then drifted off to sleep, excited about her flight to France.

CHAPTER TWELVE

She's in control now...

Two nights later... Paris, France

"Mmmm, Donavan, yaasss." Doll moaned as Donni swirled his tongue around her clit.

He had her legs lifted on the counter in the bathroom of his condo in Paris. It was high rise, and she could see the city out the small bathroom window that was wide open, letting in a cool breeze. It was four in the morning, and they had just gotten in from a lounge with a few of Donni's friends from France. They were drunk, so there was no better way to end their late night/early morning with steamy sex.

She rubbed on her nipples through her silk robe as he continued to feast. She told herself she wasn't going to give him any sex on their trip. But the way he was treating her, he was so tempting. She wasn't in love. She was horny and had the opportunity to have sex with a clean, sexy man. She was so glad her supervisor let her take an extra day off, and she had enjoyed her stay to the fullest. They had been sightseeing, had breakfast in bed, gotten French massages, and ate at the finest restaurants.

"You like that, baby? I want you to cum in my mouth," Donni said in a seductive tone as he fingered her.

"Yes, I love it. I'm about to cum," Doll said as she pushed his face further into her love box.

Donni vibrated his tongue on Doll's clit, causing her to squirt a little. Donni took it like a pro as he continued to rub her clit.

Donni stood up and wiped his face. Doll looked down and saw his throbbing penis peeping through his jeans. She bit down on her bottom lips and cuffed his dick in her hand.

"Now, I wanna feel you," Doll said as she got off the counter and slid off her robe. Donni gazed at her body and started sucking on her titties. He then carried her into the bedroom and bent her over the bed.

"Wait, you want to use a condom?" Doll asked before he entered her.

"I'm clean, and I'm sure you are too," Donni said as he slid inside of her slowly.

Doll had recently gotten all her results back, and she was definitely clean.

Feeling Donni slide inside her threw her in a trance. He filled her up nicely, and his stroke was killing Jordin's. He was stroking her slowly while he rubbed her clit as much as he could.

"Damn, Dollaysia, you feel good," Donni said seductively as he gently smacked her ass.

"I want you to fuck me harder, Donni. Go deeper," Doll said. She was craving rough sex.

Donni picked up the pace. He was fit, and he had stamina, so if she wanted rough sex, he was going to give it to her.

"Yo' knees getting weak, huh?" Donni asked as he continued to stroke her. She was moaning and sliding from under him as she gripped the sheets. Donni didn't think she knew what she was getting herself into when she said she wanted him to go deeper.

"Yes," Doll laughed.

She looked over her shoulder, and she could tell Donni was giving her his all. She tooted her ass back in the air like a pro and started throwing it back on him. Donni stopped stroking her and watched her go to work. He placed his hands behind his head like he was under arrest while she threw her ass back on him. It was turning him on the way she was looking back at him and biting her lip. He smacked her ass and then caught her same rhythm.

"That's right. Throw that ass back on me," Donni said in a seductive tone.

He felt like he was about to bust. He then laid her on her back and slid back inside of her missionary style. He kept his same fast pace as he kissed on her neck and sucked on her bottom lip. Doll wrapped her legs around his waist as he thrust in her. She sucked on his neck, giving him huge monkey bites like they were in high school.

"I'm about to bust," Donni said as he wiped sweat from his face.

"Yes, cum for me, baby. You can bust inside of me, I'm on birth control."

That was all he needed to hear. After a few more strokes, he came all inside of Doll, and it felt great. He planted a huge kiss on her lips, and she began to laugh.

"Boy, that was great. I feel good."

"I'm happy to hear that. I feel good too."

After their sexual escapade, Doll got out of bed and walked into the bathroom. She turned on the shower and then slipped in her robe. When she walked back into the room, Donni was sitting near the window in his Versace boxer briefs. He was gazing out at the Eiffel Tower. Doll smiled and walked over to him.

"It's so beautiful looking out this window; it's like a dream for me," Doll said, snapping out him out his thoughts.

"Yes, it is. I felt the same way when I first got my condo here last year."

"Thank you for letting me come here. I was so scared at first, but I figured I should live for me now and stop worrying about how others feel."

"No problem. A beautiful woman like you deserves the world." Donni stood up and wrapped his arms around her.

"If you are just with me for my looks, having sex in Paris is probably as far as we're going to go." Doll broke away from their hug.

"Dollaysia, you are more than looks. You are a gem, inside and out. Our relationship will go beyond this one trip and sex. Just trust in me." He gazed in her eyes, hoping she would believe him. Donni had never been so sure about a woman until he encountered Doll. She was everything he wanted and needed. He wanted to take her away from the broken marriage she was in and place her in a healthy environment.

"Yeah, that's what my husband said." Doll walked off and headed to the bathroom. She didn't know what to believe anymore. It was as though men had a secret handbook, and they all used the same lines. She wanted to believe him, but she knew only time would tell.

After she showered, she put on a pair of boy shorts and a bra. By the time she stepped out the bathroom, Donni was asleep. She walked toward the bed and got under the covers with him. She gazed out at the sun coming up, thinking about so much. She didn't understand why she craved love so much, and she was hoping Donni would love her. But she wasn't going to show him too much. She was vulnerable for Jordin, and she didn't want to be that way with Donni. She wanted to show him the strong side of her. She had shown Jordin her weakness, and he took it for granted. That was something she wasn't going to let happen again.

"I hope you're not like my ex," Doll said as she stroked his face. She then drifted off to sleep.

$$$$$

Five hours later, Doll was riding in the back of a black Rolls Royce with Donni on their way to the diamond district. She looked over at him, and he was gazing out the window. He had on a pair of Versace shades, a pair of beige slacks, and a white, button-up shirt. She then glanced at his shoes. He was wearing a pair of black Gucci loafers with no socks.

Only rich niggas wear no socks with their loafers. She snickered to herself and put her mind of where they were headed. She remembered when her mother would always say that when they went shopping around rich people.

She had four hours left until it was time for them to fly back, and she wasn't leaving without buying a nice piece of jewelry from Paris. She had bought so many clothes, and she let Donni buy her a few pieces as well. She didn't want him cashing out on her just because he had money. Inviting her was just enough for her. She had her own money, so she splurged a little bit.

"You're always in your own little world. What do you be thinking about?" Doll asked, breaking him out of his thoughts.

Donni took off his shades and looked at Doll. "I'm always thinking about ways to better myself. I have so many business deals on the line that I can't stop thinking about. Why you ask that, though?" he asked, taking an interest in why she wanted to know about his constant daydreaming.

"Because you're always staring off in space, stroking your chin hairs. I just wanted to get in your head for a minute. That's all. See what you be thinking about," she smiled.

"If you ever want to know anything about me, don't ever hesitate to ask. I'll be honest with you every time."

"I hope so …"

"Stop right here, driver," Donni said quickly, as the driver was passing up their destination while they were talking.

His driver pulled over in front of a jewelry store. They stepped out of the car and walked into the store. When they walked in, Doll's eyes lit up. She felt like she was a little girl in a candy shop. Everything sparkled off the bright lights that were shining brightly in their showroom.

"Everything here is so beautiful," Doll said as her eyes locked to a beautiful diamond and emerald necklace. It looked like something that belonged on a queen's or princess's neck.

"So you like that necklace?" Donni asked when he walked over to Doll as she gazed at the necklace he knew she wanted.

"Yes, I love it. But I can't afford a thirty-grand necklace," Doll said in a bitter tone.

"Excuse me, ma'am. Can you pull this necklace out and let her see it? Once she's done, you can wrap it up and charge me," Donni said to the woman working behind the counter. She smiled and opened the case.

"Okay, sir," the woman said with her French accent.

"Oh no, Donavan. I can't let you buy me this necklace. That's way too much money, and we're not even a couple. You know I'm still married, and—"

Donni cut her off. "Look, Dollaysia. I have enough money in my account to buy you two of these and just walk away from you, but I'd never do that to you. I have $10 million sitting in my bank right now just from memberships at my gyms. That's ten times more than what your drug dealer husband is making. I'm nothing like that punk ass nigga and never will be. My money is legit, my heart is genuine, and I'm set for the rest of my life. And you will be too if you just let a nigga in your world. I'm thirty-one years old. I don't want to waste no more of my life dating; I'm looking for something long term."

Doll gazed at him and then gazed at the necklace. It was like déjà vu times ten when Jordin bought her a necklace with her engagement ring on it. Jordin had money, but he had nowhere near $10 million sitting in his bank, and if he did, it wasn't legal money. He had never bought her anything over $10,000, and when he did, it was because he had fucked up, and Doll was on her way to leave him. Donni was buying her this necklace out of the kindness of his heart and because he could do that every day if he wanted to. Therefore, she decided not to pass up this opportunity.

"Okay, I'll let you buy me the necklace, but we still have a long way before I completely let you in my world."

Donni kissed her forehead. "I'll take that."

The jeweler smiled and handed Doll the necklace. It was a bit heavy, and she loved the rose gold that the diamonds and emeralds were sitting in. After the jeweler wrapped up her necklace, Doll still ended up purchasing another necklace that cost way less with a matching bracelet, and Donni bought himself a few gold chains. After shopping, they had a quick lunch and headed back to Donni's condo to get ready for their flight back to Los Angeles.

As Doll packed her bags, she became depressed. She knew she was going back to the States to a broken marriage that probably was going to take all of her soul to get out of.

"You okay?" Donni asked, noticing her wiping a tear that was falling from her eye.

"I'm such a big baby. I just don't want to leave this place," she smiled.

Donni chuckled and then took her in for a hug. "You don't have to cry about it, lil' mama. Whenever you get some more time off and want to get away, you can. I'm always free to fly out."

Doll's single tear turned into whimpers. Something about his hug and the way he was being so sincere broke her down. She wished it were him that she was married to all those years. She wished that she could just give him her heart, and they could live happily ever after, but she knew she had to take her time. She had a wall up, and she didn't want to take it down for Donni, even though she knew it was okay to do so. She knew anything could happen, and the love and attention he was showing her could go away. So that was what was pushing her away.

Donni rubbed her back as he felt her tears seep through the arm of his shirt. His heart broke for her. He knew she was going through a lot and knew she was going to have to face whatever she was going through when she got back.

"I don't understand why he treats me like I'm his property and not his wife. He cheated on me our whole marriage, and I couldn't do anything, not even hang with my friends. Everyone knew he was cheating on me. I feel like a damn fool!" Doll cried out, letting her weakness seep through. She just couldn't help it. She just couldn't hold back her hurt any longer, and Donavan was there, letting her cry on his shoulder. He did not see her as weak; he saw a strong woman with a broken heart. He saw a woman that trusted her husband to love her, and he failed.

"Some niggas just don't know what they have, Doll. But I know you are more than just some damn property. I know you deserve better. And whenever you are with me, I'll show you what you are worth. I can only speak for myself, not that nigga, though."

"Once this is all over, I'm going to make time for you, Donavan. I promise. Just wait for me to get my life back on track again." She kissed him on the lips.

"I'll wait for you forever, babe. That's how much I'm serious about you. Now let's get out of here. Our plane is waiting, and I have an important meeting when I touch down. We will hook up in a couple days to hang out. Take ya mind off the bullshit."

"Thank you."

They finished packing and rushed off to catch their flight.

$$$$$

The Following Day...

Doll sat in the back of PF Chang's in Beverly Hills, waiting on Breann. She was so angry at Breann at first, but her time in Paris made her realize that it wasn't Breann's fault Jordin was cheating on her. Breann was right; she had told Doll from the beginning that she shouldn't have hooked up with Jordin, but she went with her heart and did it anyway. She truly loved Jordin and went with his word. But now she wished she had listened to Breann. All the signs were there that he was having an affair with Tiffany, but her love for him blinded her.

Doll looked up from the Mojito and saw Breann walking up. She looked flawless in her black one-piece pantsuit and white Ferragamo heels. She was smiling ear to ear as her long ponytail swung from left to right.

"What's up, boo? You look rich as fuck!" Breann said loudly as she checked out Doll's appearance. What caught her eye the most was her diamond and emerald necklace she was wearing. It was shining brightly and looked like it cost a bunch of money. Breann knew costume jewelry when she saw it, and that, it wasn't.

"Bitch, me? You look flawless. I love that ponytail."

"Thank you." Breann sat down and picked up the menu.

"So where have you been. You look different. Last time I saw you, you looked stressed out," Breann said.

"I've been in Paris with Donni," she smiled.

"*Paris with Donni?* Girl, spill it. How did you find him again?" Breann was smiling brightly.

"He left his card when he somehow ended up at Jordin's shop, but that's another story. We had dinner one night in his office, and he invited me on the trip. He's a fucking millionaire, best friend. I've been acting like I don't care about him being paid, but I do. He has a condo in Paris, and he owns three gyms. He's on some legit shit and way past Jordin's level. I really think he's into me too. He bought me this $30K necklace." Doll moved in closer so Breann could see her necklace.

"Bitch, of course he's into you! You're a beautiful person, inside and out, so don't let that nigga, Jordin, make you feel no different. It's still good men out there. You done came up from Jordin's raggedy ass almost overnight, and I am happy for you. But I need to fill you in on what's going on. Shit is ugly. Jordin is on a rampage, looking for you …"

"I talked to him. I'm supposed to meet with him, but I don't know. I'm kind of scared."

"You need to be scared … Word around is he killed Tiffany. But nobody knows for sure. But she was wheeled out her apartment in a body bag. Somebody said she was choked to death in her shower." Breann shook her head. "But that could have been anybody with the reputation she has."

"Damn … that's creepy. Well, thanks for the heads up. I also want to apologize for being mad at you. It wasn't your fault, and I truly understand why you didn't warn me again. Jordin is crazy."

"I'm glad you understand. I wished every day I could have told you. I should have disguised the shit," she laughed.

"Well, I know now. He has the divorce papers already. He said he's not signing them."

"I'm sure his dog ass isn't. Well, let's eat. I'm starving!" Breann said as she slammed her menu down.

The two ordered a feast of Chinese food and drinks.

CHAPTER THIRTEEN

Give me another chance...

Five Days Later ...

$\mathcal{D}$onni pulled in front of Doll's apartment building and killed his engine. He then looked over at her and smiled. They had just come from his gym, working out. She loved working out with Donni. It felt good, and she felt like they were building a bond through wellness. She liked that, and she didn't mind doing it every other day before she went to work.

"I enjoyed my workout and dinner with you," Donni said with a smile. They had just come from his gym and did a little kickboxing training and then had another vegan dinner.

"I did too. I'm going to be energized at work. But I'm going to crash when I get home."

"That's good. Sleep is a part of a healthy lifestyle."

"I know, you've been keeping me in line all week with my health. I appreciate it. It's bringing my stress levels down a lot. I'll call you in the morning so you can come over and chill." She reached over and kissed him.

"That's cool. You've been to my condo in Paris. One day, when you are ready, I can bring you to my house."

Doll laughed. "What? You're tired of hanging in my ran-down condo?"

"Your condo is nice. And hanging with you always humbles me. You let me know that there's more to life other than cash and cars."

She smiled. "That's good to know."

Doll stepped out of his Bentley and walked onto the curb. When he drove off, she proceeded to walk to the front entrance of her condo. Before she could put her key in the glass door, she felt somebody snatch her arm and put their hand over her mouth before she could scream. The person dragged her away. Doll was struggling to break away from the man, but she failed. When they made it to the man's car, she finally saw who it was when he hit the locks on his brand-new Mercedes truck. Jordin pushed her in his passenger seat and slammed the door. He then locked it and then rushed over to the driver's seat.

"Jordin, you got me fucked up! Let me out of here!" Doll shouted as she tried to unlock the door before he drove off.

Jordin shoved her back into her seat aggressively as he drove off.

"Sit the fuck back. I'm taking you home with me," Jordin said aggressively.

"I don't live there, Jordin. And this is kidnapping!"

"You're my wife! You think you're going to go run off with some rich nigga? I been watching your ass; you're not going nowhere."

Jordin did one hundred on the freeway to Pomona. Doll was furious, and if she had a gun, she would've killed him. He was out of line for snatching her up, and she wanted out of the situation.

"If you don't pull over, I'm going to jump out. I'd rather die than be with you," Doll said in a serious tone.

Jordin chuckled. "Is that right?"

Before he knew it, Doll took her fist and punched him in the face. "I fucking hate you, Jordin! You can't run my life. I don't want to be with you! You're about to make me lose my job. I swear to God. I fucking hate you!" Doll shouted as she continued to throw punches at him. Every blow she gave him, she meant it from the pit of her soul. She was taking all her anger out on him, and she didn't care if they crashed.

Jordin pulled over on the side of the road so he wouldn't crash. He tried pushing her away and grabbing her hands, but it didn't work. That was when she took her foot and kicked him in his side so hard hat it caught him off guard. He slapped her so hard that her face hit the window.

Doll screamed in agony, but that didn't stop her from fighting him. She started scratching his face. Jordin grabbed her by her throat and held her down. He didn't want to choke her like he had done Tiffany, but he was tired and angry. His shirt was ripped, and he had blood leaking from his lip.

"I swear to God that I'd fight 'til death with you, Dollaysia. I love you, and I don't want you to leave me. Please don't leave me, babe,"

Jordin said as he looked in Doll's pleading eyes. She was fighting for air, but Jordin wasn't letting her go. "If I can't have you, nobody can have you. Fuck that nigga. I'll murder him," was the last thing Doll heard Jordin say before she blacked out …

$$$$$

Five a.m....

Dollie woke up in her old bed. She felt groggy and didn't know how she even got to her old house.

Did I get drunk last night and come to the wrong house? Doll asked herself. That was when it hit her when Jordin came in the room in his underwear. She sat up quickly.

"Good morning. You were out for a few hours. I'm glad you're up. I thought I was going to have to take you to the hospital, but you started breathing." Jordin stood over the bed and gazed at her.

She looked under the cover, and she was naked. She gasped. "Did you have sex with me after I blacked out after you choked me?" Doll asked as she looked at him. She was starting to remember everything that had happened the night before. She was supposed to go to work, but Jordin had snatched her. She knew she had to be fired by now, and that angered her to the core.

"Nah, I would never do that to you. I took your clothes off and put you in bed. Look, I'm sorry about that. I just get crazy over you. I don't want you to leave me. And I'm not signing those papers or letting you go until we try and work this out."

"Jordin, it's over … We can't keep pretending like we can make things work, and we can't. You couldn't even make it through the whole ninety days before all your secrets started coming out. You were with Tiffany before me and during our marriage. She was pregnant by you and gave you a STD, some stuff just can't be forgiven." She got out of bed and walked over to the closet she once shared with Jordin. She had left a lot of stuff behind, and Jordin hadn't touched a thing since she left. She found one of her t-shirts and shorts. She slipped it on and sat back on the bed. She looked over at Jordin. He had his head down, looking at the floor.

"Well, I'm not letting you go until you make love to me one last time, and we live like a couple one last time. If you don't do that, I'll never sign those papers, and neither of us might not make it out of here alive." He turned around and looked at her with an evil look on his face. His look sent chills up her arms because she knew how deadly he could get.

"Did you kill Tiffany, Jordin?" Doll stood up.

"Yeah, I killed her for you. I killed her for us, babe. We can move on and be happy." He stood up and walked over to her. Doll backed away from him as he moved closer to her. She backed up so far that her back hit the dresser.

"So you're scared of me now? I'm your husband, Dollaysia. And I'm not letting anyone take that from me." He grabbed her face and planted a sloppy, wet kiss on her lips.

She pushed him away. "You're fucking crazy. You got two days with me, and then I want those papers signed and you out my life!" She grabbed her purse from the nightstand and stormed into the restroom.

"Be ready in an hour, beautiful. I have a full day planned for us,"

Jordin said with a chuckle as he lay back on the bed. He grabbed his blunt and lighter from his nightstand and lit it.

Two days, my ass …

Meanwhile, Doll sat on the toilet with a face full of tears. Jordin had taken her against her will, and she contemplated calling the police. But she didn't want to drag out a kidnapping case and getting her family involved. She was just going to be with him for a couple of days, get the papers signed, and go. Hearing that he killed Tiffany made her sick to her stomach. She didn't like Tiffany, but she never wished death on her. She probably was a victim just as much as Doll was since she had been with him longer. She scrolled through her phone that was dying and saw that she had a few missed calls from Donni. That made her cry more. She knew he probably was thinking she was avoiding him, and that wasn't the case. She decided to send him a text. But not a regular text. It was something like a cry for help.

"Hey, Donni, sorry I have been missing your calls. But I need you to do me a favor. If I don't call you in two days at five in the morning, please come to this address and find me as soon as you can. 234 Pepperwood Circle. It's in Pomona."

Donni texted back immediately.

Donavan: "What's going on, Dollaysia? Why can't I come now? You got me worried as fuck, lil' mama."

"It's my ex. Just do what I say, please. Don't come any sooner than two days, and don't call me, okay? Promise me."

Donavan: "Yeah, I promise. But I'll kill that nigga if he hurts you.

Call me."

Boom, boom, boom!

"I don't hear no water running!" Jordin shouted as he banged on the door.

I'll call you. She stuffed her phone in her purse and turned on the shower.

Doll showered and then headed back into the room. She walked into the closet and found a pair of jeans and a shirt. She then slipped on her Fenty slippers she had left behind and then headed downstairs. When she walked downstairs, Jordin was sitting on the couch. He had his keys in his hand and a duffle bag sitting at his foot.

"I'm ready. Now where are we going?" Doll asked with a slight attitude.

"We're going to Laughlin where we spent our honeymoon."

Doll rolled her eyes in the air. She knew he was going to try and rekindle the love they had when they first got married. But she was so turned off by his actions. Jordin was not the man she thought she married. He was Mercy, and there was no way she was going to be with him. However, she was going to play his game so she could get what she wanted, and that was a divorce.

They got into Jordin's car and headed for the road to Laughlin …

$$$$$

Five hours later, they were pulling into a Laughlin mall so Doll could buy clothes for their overnight stay, and then they were headed to the hotel Jordin had booked for them. However, he took a detour after they left the mall and headed toward the mountains. Doll noticed they were driving a little too far out, so she became curious.

"Where are we going?" Doll asked, not taking her eyes off him.

"You'll see," Jordin said with a smirk on his face

Ten minutes later, Doll looked out the window and Jordin had brought them to a bungee jumping area. Doll always wanted to go bungee jumping, but Jordin was too afraid. As hard as he was in the streets, he was truly afraid of heights. He didn't get on rollercoasters, and he damn sure didn't bungee jump. But today, he was going to take a risk.

"Jordin, what are we doing here? You know you are afraid of heights."

"Not anymore. I remember when you saw this when we were here on our honeymoon, and I refused to go up there and jump with you. But today, I want to show you that I will do anything for you." He proceeded to open the door.

Doll's heart was jumping out her chest. She knew how afraid he was of heights, and she didn't want him doing anything that was going to kill him. She knew fear killed people, and she didn't want Jordin diving and dying on her watch.

"I don't think I'm ready to do this, Jordin."

"You're scared now? You were so pumped four years ago. Now look at you," he poked at her, causing her to laugh a little.

"Come on, boy. If you have a heart attack, don't blame me." She opened the door.

Jordin laughed. "I won't."

Dollie slipped on the fresh pair of Nikes she had gotten from the mall, and she and Jordin headed off to the line.

As they stood in line, Jordin hugged Doll from behind as he kissed on her neck. Doll let him. As much as he hated him, she knew pushing him away would only cause problems, so she let him feel like they were a happy couple.

"I want this forever, Doll. I'm going to show you that I can be the husband you want me to be."

Doll ignored him ...

A few minutes later, they were in the front of the line, waiting to be strapped to a rope. Doll looked down and swallowed the lump in her throat. She was nervous, and she wasn't sure if she even wanted to jump. They were so high up, and she had never jumped before. When she first married Jordin, she was full of life, and trusted him with everything. Now she couldn't see herself jumping off a cliff with a man she no longer loved. But she knew she had to do it.

"Ma'am, are you ready?" the man asked as he handed Doll a helmet to put on. She looked over at Jordin, and he was smiling from ear to ear.

"Yes, she's ready, sir. Strap her up!" Jordin said with excitement.

Doll shook her head. "You really are crazy, boy."

"Crazy for you," he planted a kiss on her lips.

"So will you two be going down together or separate?" the man asked.

"Together," Jordin answered.

Jordin and Doll were strapped together, chest to chest. They were then walked to the edge of the cliff.

"You said you would rather die than be with me, so if we die, you won't have to worry about me anymore." He smiled as they looked each other in the eyes while they were strapped chest to chest.

"We're not going to die, and I didn't mean that, Jordin. Stop it."

"You don't know what's going to happen. Do you trust me to keep you safe on our way down?" Jordin asked with a serious look on his face.

"Yes, I trust you to save me. But I don't trust you with my heart anymore. You are only the protector of my flesh and not my heart."

Jordin shook his head. "Aight, Doll. You got it." Doll was hurting his feelings by the minute, but he was going to continue to try and win her back.

The attendant walked them to the ledge and counted to three. Once he got to three, he pushed them off the edge. The three-hundred-foot fall had Doll's heart in her throat as she let out a scream. Jordin laughed as he held her tight as they went down.

"If you die, baby, I'ma die with you. We're in this together," Jordin joked with a smile on his face.

"Shut up, Jordin!" Doll shouted with her eyes closed.

"Open your eyes! The scenery is dope!" Jordin said.

Doll opened her eyes as they were bouncing around on the thin rope. He was right; the scene was beautiful. There was a river next to them along with huge mountain rocks surrounding them. She took a deep breath and calmed her nerves.

"See, babe. I faced my fear, and little do you know, you faced yours to. That's how our relationship is. It's rocky, but you know we can bounce back if you just face your fears and love me again," Jordin said in a sincere tone as they were brought back up.

"I hear you, Jordin ..."

Once they were back on the top of the cliff, they were unstrapped, and Jordin paid the man for their jump. They then got into his car and headed for the hotel. When they pulled up, Doll looked out the window and saw that they were about to check into the same Hilton they spent their honeymoon in. She remembered it like yesterday. She remembered how much of a gentleman Jordin was back then. He had opened her door for her and carried her inside to their penthouse suite for the week.

"We're going to spend the night in the same room we made love in."

Jordin grabbed all their bags from his trunk, and they let valet park his car. They walked into the hotel, and they walked up to the desk.

"I have a reservation for your penthouse suite. Here's my driver's license to confirm." Jordin pulled out his wallet and handed the receptionist his license. "And send two bottles of Clicquot Rose to our room."

The woman smiled and handed him two room keys. When they walked into the room, they both started getting comfortable. Doll walked into the bathroom and turned on the jacuzzi tub and filled it with hot water and bubbles. Jordin turned on some music while he rolled a blunt. As her water ran, Doll slipped out of her clothes in front of Jordin and started digging in her new clothes for the black teddy Jordin insisted that she wore for the night. She agreed. She wasn't going to kick up any dust about any of his demands, because she wanted their trip to go smoothly and be over.

"Your body's sexy as fuck. Looks like you been working that ass out a lot. I can't wait to get up in that," Jordin said as he licked his blunt together.

"Yeah, I bet. Hurry up with that blunt and bring that bottle of champagne in the bathroom when it comes. I'm trying to get fucked up before I fuck you to sleep, *husband*." She sashayed off into the bathroom and closed the door.

"Yeah, aight ... *wifey* ..."

Five minutes later, room service had brought their liquor, and Jordin headed to the bathroom with Doll. When he walked in, Doll was laid back in the tub with her hair all curly over her head. He stood in the doorway, gazing at her as she lay in her own world, humming to the music. Jordin knew he had fucked up with her, and he knew she wasn't going to be with him. But he was going to drag their marriage out for as long as he could. He knew Doll was beautiful inside and out and deserved someone better. But his selfish ways just wouldn't let him let her go. Jordin lit his blunt and walked over to the jacuzzi.

"I got your bottle," Jordin said, snapping her out her thoughts.

"Well, open it up and pass me that blunt."

Jordin chuckled. "You're real demanding tonight. That rich nigga got you cocky." He popped the bottle and let all the bubbles fall down his arm. He then took a sip.

"Nah, what got me cocky is that I'm surviving a broken marriage and heartache with my head held high."

"Look, Doll, I'm sorry about the way things are ending. I want to fix shit, but you won't let me."

"The damage is already done. Now let's enjoy our last night. You're killing a bitch's vibe with all that begging." Doll pulled on the blunt and let smoke come out her nose. She just wanted to relax and not listen to Jordin beg for forgiveness for the millionth time.

Jordin shook his head and passed her the bottle of champagne.

After two blunts and a bottle and a half of champagne, Doll found herself in doggy style with Jordin licking her from her clit to her crack. He was going up and down her backside with his tongue, making her moan out his name. Jordin opened her ass cheeks and let his tongue penetrate her hole. Doll was enjoying every moment of it. One thing she liked about Jordin was he was nasty. He would lick her ass and then turn around and drink her cum. She didn't know how freaky Donni was yet, because they only had sex once, but she knew this was something she was going to miss if Donni wasn't a freak like her.

"You like that, Doll? You want me to stop?" Jordin asked in a drunken yet seductive tone. The liquor and weed had him gone, and he was going to do whatever Doll said.

"No, keep going," Doll said as she looked back at him. She really didn't want any dick, so she was going to prolong it for as long as she could. But she knew Jordin was going to be ready to dig her out soon.

Jordin then laid her on her back and pushed her legs to her head. He dove in face first again, going at her clit with his tongue. Doll pushed his face in deeper as he continued to play with her clit. Her temperature began to rise, and before she knew it, she was squirting so hard Jordin had to move back because it was impossible to catch it all.

"Damn, I love when you squirt. That shit turns me on," Jordin said as he stroked his hard dick that was peeping out his boxers.

"Go get the condoms we bought and put one on," Doll said as she rubbed her clit.

Jordin went over to the dresser and pulled one of the condoms out the box. He slid it on his dick and walked over to Doll. He couldn't believe he now had to use a condom with his own wife. He remembered how good she felt without a condom. Now he was restricted from fully feeling her. He brushed off his thoughts and climbed on the bed.

Doll had rolled onto her stomach, ready for him to hit her from behind. She didn't want to make love to him; she wanted to fuck. She felt like if she looked him in the eyes, it would become too emotional, especially for Jordin. She didn't want to feel any emotions on her last ride with him. She was done, and he wasn't going to win her heart with sex ever again.

Jordin slid inside of her slowly as he gripped her ass and watched her juices flow. Her pussy was making farting sounds as he went deep inside of her.

"Oohh, Jordin, fuck me good," Doll said with her face in the pillow, boosting his ego so he could nut.

Jordin smacked her ass and then picked up the pace. He was giving her the business, and he knew it. He had Doll clenching the sheets and moaning out his name in ecstasy.

"You gonna miss this dick? You gonna miss daddy?" Jordin asked as he slammed his pelvis into her ass. He was working up a sweat and getting a little tired, but he kept going.

"Yes, I'm going to miss this dick, Jordin!" Doll shouted as he continued to give her long strokes just the way she liked it.

Jordin was hitting her spot and had tears flowing from her eyes. But she wiped her face before he could see them. He had bruised her heart and broke down her down. The only thing the man she married had to offer was dick. That made her angry, but the pleasure he was giving her was so good. She started throwing her ass back on him, trying to bring him to his peak, and sure enough, he did.

Jordin pulled off the condom and skeeted his seed on her ass. Doll collapsed, and so did Jordin. His head was spinning from all the liquor in his system, but he felt great. He could hardly move or mutter a word. He closed his eyes and drifted off to sleep. Doll heard him snoring. Her mission was complete. She stood from bed and walked into the bathroom of their suite. She took a shower and slipped back on her teddy. She lay next to Jordin as he continued to sleep in the nude.

"You're sexy, but you ain't mine anymore. I'm done with you," Doll said as she continued to gaze at his tattooed chest and scarred-up stomach from being shot. She was finally leaving Jordin, and she was happy about it. Doll turned off the light and fell asleep next to Jordin for the last time …

CHAPTER FOURTEEN

There is no more us...

One day later ...

$\mathcal{D}$onni sat his phone down on his coffee table and sighed. He couldn't stop reading the text he had gotten from Doll the morning before, and he couldn't get her off his mind. However, he had to move on with his day yet again.

I'ma have to kill this nigga, he thought as he walked into his kitchen to make some eggs.

As he was making his eggs, he turned on his Spotify app on his Bluetooth speaker. Gucci Mane's song "Bucket List" started blaring through his living room. He had a long day ahead of himself, so he needed to pump himself up. He made his eggs, poured some orange juice, and then sat to eat his food. He bobbed his head to his loud music and looked through a fitness magazine as he ate.

I need to put a magazine together myself, Donni thought as he flipped through the pages.

Donni finished up his food and sat his plate in the sink. He slid out his shirt and tossed it on the couch before heading to his bathroom to shower. As he was walking off, he heard his doorbell ring. He turned down his music and walked to the door. When he looked out the peephole, it was Lisha.

Shit, he thought to himself.

"I know you're in there, nigga. I hear your music. Let me in, I need to talk to you!" Lisha shouted on the other side of the door.

Not wanting her to cause a scene, he sighed and then opened the door. As soon as it opened, Lisha walked in and brushed past him. Donni shook his head and closed the door.

"Just because we're broken up and fucking someone else doesn't mean you can't call me and check on the baby."

"I was going to call you," Donni mumbled as he flopped on the couch. He turned on his TV and found the ESPN channel for highlights. He wasn't in the mood to deal with Lisha. He had Dollaysia on his mind heavy, and he almost had forgotten about his situation with Lisha. There wasn't too much he could do since she wasn't due anytime soon. But he never thought about how she would be demanding his attention while she was pregnant.

"No, you weren't, so who did you go to Paris with? That girl you had in your office last week?" Lisha flopped on his loveseat and crossed her legs. Donni looked at her appearance. She was dressed in a gray cotton dress, showing off her new baby bump. He shook his head.

"That's none of your business ..."

"Um ... Well, she looks poor. Does she know you're an ex-hitman turned millionaire?" Lisha asked with a smirk on her face.

"And you have money?" he raised his eyebrow.

"Actually, I don't. And since you're my baby daddy, I think it's time for us to get the child support going."

Donni laughed. "You're letting your gold digging ways shine these days, huh? I won't be agreeing to any child support arrangements until the child is born." He stood up.

Lisha stood up, furious. "Why! Do you know how much it costs me every time I go to the damn doctor to check on the baby? I don't have money coming in like that, Donavan!"

"I thought you had a new job, Lisha? That's what you told me."

"I lied because you had that bitch in there, making me look like some crazy baby mama!"

"Well, that's how you are acting, Lisha. Like some crazy, gold digging ass baby mama. Now I can help you with your doctor bills, but I can't take care of you financially. You need to put one of those degrees to use and stop living off me."

Lisha looked Donni up and down. He was shirtless, and the print that was seeping from his sweats, giving her life. As much as she wanted to do her own thing, she couldn't help but crave what Donni had in between his legs. She gazed at his washboard abs and strong arms. Donni was something special, and she never understood why he couldn't keep her full attention. Lisha walked up to him and massaged his print threw his sweats.

"Well, can I take care of your needs when your girl isn't around?

And then I can earn my money that way," Lisha said as she continued to massage his stick. She felt it growing and wanted a taste. But Donni moved her hand away. He wasn't interested in anything she had to offer.

"I don't have to pay for it, Lisha, and you know that. I got a lot of shit to do today, so if you're done here, you can leave."

Lisha backed away. "I see it's like that, huh? Okay ... Well, since you want to have it your way, I'm going to make sure I ask for the highest amount of child support I can get when the time comes. Enjoy your day, *rich boy*." Lisha threw her hair to her back and headed for the door.

"Yeah, okay ... Lock the door on your way out, and next time, call before you just come to my crib!" Donni shouted. The door slammed. "Stupid ass bitch," Donni said as he walked into his bathroom. He turned on his shower and slipped out the rest of his clothing. He stepped in the steaming water and let his waterfall shower head fall over his wavy hair. He started wondering what was going on with Doll.

I hope he isn't hurting her, he thought to himself. If I have to show up in two days, I'm going to have to bring out the old me, he thought again.

Before Donavan became successful, he came from a hard place. Donni was born and raised in Oakland, California, and all he knew was getting money. But for as long as he could remember, he was always into fitness and sports. He had been in shape since he started high school and started playing every sport the school had to offer. But to make ends meet, he had to hang with his cousins to get money for the family. Donni decided to be a part of the contracted killer team with his cousin Stacey. He wasn't into selling drugs, but he could deal with blood on his hands from somebody that was probably disloyal. Donni saved all his money from his jobs, but when he became an adult, the street life followed, so he couldn't get out the game as fast as he intended. However, he managed to get his degree in exercise science, nutrition specialist, and physical education. After finally calling it quits as a hitman when he twenty-nine, he opened his first gym, and his business took off fast because of all the knowledge he knew about the fitness industry. Now, he owned three with a deal on the line that could change his life forever. He was looking to open a gym in every state and start franchises and even expand to France.

I'm going to get her back and make her mine ... She's going to live the good life with me.

Donni got out the shower and started his day ...

$$\$\$\$\$\$\$$$

After Donni's full day at his gym, having meeting after meeting, he walked out to his Porsche and hit the locks. When he got in, he sat behind his wheel, looking at his phone at Doll's text message. He wanted to call her to make sure she was okay, but he didn't want to go against her word.

She's probably okay, he tried to convince himself.

He then went out her texts and sent his cousin Stacey a text.

"I'm on my way, bro. I need to talk to you about some shit."

Big Bro Stacey: *"Aight, just pull in my driveway and lock the gate."*

"Fasho..."

Donni started his car and let the engine roar. He stepped on the gas once and then turned on his music. He backed out of his stall and headed to the east side of Los Angeles to vent to his cousin Stacey. He and Stacey had been tight since birth. They were blood cousins and tighter than ever even though Stacey chose to still live the street life. He and Donni always stayed in contact and hung out like brothers. Therefore, he knew he could trust him with any information he gave him. Fifteen minutes later, Donni pulled in front of his cousin's house. It was a nice family home that was gated with a two-car garage. Stacey had money, but he preferred to live in the hood. When he and Donni moved to Los Angeles to do business, Stacey decided to move to the east side of LA because it reminded him of Oakland.

Donni stepped out of his car and walked through the gate. He then knocked on the door, and his cousin Stacey opened the door. Stacey was smiling ear to ear when he laid eyes on his cousin.

"Look at you, my nigga. I see you shining. I see them diamonds in ya ears," Stacey said with excitement as he gave his cousin daps. "That corporate life looks good on you, my nigga," Stacey said as they walked into the living room.

"Good looking out. A nigga had a few meetings today, so I had to dress accordingly for these French motherfuckers. I'm trying to open a gym in Paris." Donni flopped on the couch and loosened his tie.

"That's what's up, doing big thangs. I'm glad you stopped by though. You want a shot of something?"

"Yeah, bring the whole fuckin' bottle, bro." Donni kicked off his loafers, leaving on his socks. He always got comfortable when he went to his cousin's.

Stacey laughed. "Fasho, bro."

Stacey walked back into the living room and sat two tall shot glasses down and bottle of Hennessey.

"Man, tell me you know a nigga name Jordin from Compton. I guess they call him Mercy. The nigga owns a weed shop on Compton Boulevard." Donni poured his first shot.

Stacey stroked his chin as he thought on the name. "Bro, that's the nigga we *didn't* take out for that nigga Janario on the last two jobs we did four years ago. The nigga lived—the nigga we popped over there in them projects on 118th Place. I guess that was too long ago for you," Stacey chuckled.

"Oh shit … For dude that wanted to take his own homie out over some money? Nigga, I came a long way from taking niggas out for a living. I forgot who I killed or didn't kill. Well, we might have our chance. This nigga is married to this chick I'm fuckin with heavy. Like I want to marry this girl. Her and that nigga going through a divorce. But she texted me yesterday, saying if she doesn't call me by 5:00 a.m. tomorrow, she wants me to come get her. She texted me the address." Donni took his iPhone 8 out his pocket and pulled up her text. He then handed his phone to Stacey.

Stacey shook his head as he read the text. "Damn, so you want me to ride out with you? Shit seems like it might get ugly."

"Yeah, man. This shit is driving me crazy. I'm about to be up until she calls." Donni took his shot of liquor and started pouring another.

"You know I got you, bro. The wife and kids are out of town, so

I'm up with you. I got some new burners too. You can pick ya poison when it's time." Stacey pulled his blunt from his ear and lit it.

"Fasho."

Donni and Stacey smoked and drank until the wee hours of the night, thinking of a plan to get Doll back to him. The way she cried in his arms in Paris, he knew she just wanted to be loved, and he wanted to be the one to love and protect her. Therefore, if she needed him to rescue her from her so-called husband, he was going to do it.

CHAPTER FIFTEEN

$\mathscr{D}$onni sat behind his desk with his eyes on the clock that was hanging on his wall. It was four thirty in the morning, and he was waiting for Doll to call, and she hadn't. It was day two, and he was becoming impatient. He knew there had to be a reason why she said to come get her in two days, so he wasn't going to let her down.

"It's almost five. You want to just start driving up there?" Stacey asked as his eyes pierced Donni. He had been up with his cousin on and off, anticipating Doll's call.

"Yeah, since she hasn't called. Let's go."

That was when Stacey pulled out the pieces he had in a duffle bag.

"I just bought some fire ass shit, so pick which one you want," Stacey said as he pulled out the first 9mm gun.

"That muthafucka's clean right there. You got a .38?" Donni asked. That was one of his favorite guns.

"Yup, I brought that one just for you." Stacey cocked back the empty gun and passed it to Donni.

"This will do right here. That nigga didn't die last time. But his bitch ass is gonna die today if he hurts Dollaysia, and that's my word." Donni picked up the box of bullets and opened it. He then slid his bullets in and stood from his desk.

He and Stacey left out the back of his gym and got into his Bentley truck. Donni then did ninety on the freeway to Pomona to find Dollaysia …

$$$$$$

It was four thirty in the morning when Doll sat at Jordin's kitchen table, fully dressed, with a few bags next to her feet, ready to leave. His two days were up, so it was time for him to sign their papers so she could leave. She knew Donni would be calling, and she wanted to get to him before he came to her. She knew Jordin was going to be pissed that his time had come to an end, but she had to do what was best for her. She couldn't deny the fact that she had a good time with him in Laughlin, but that wasn't enough for her to fall in love again. She'd rather Jordin move on and find someone and treat them the way they deserved. Jordin had burnt his bridges, and there was no turning back. She was ready to move on with Donni, and if he weren't the one, she was going to move on alone.

Jordin walked into the dining room and stopped in the doorway. He gazed at Doll, and then he gazed at the paper and pen that were sitting in the middle of the table. He frowned. He thought after their two days in Laughlin and love making, they were going to continue to work out their marriage. But he was sadly mistaken. Doll was ready to end their relationship and move on with her life. He had kidnapped her, and her boss already emailed her and told her she was terminated. Jordin had wrecked her life, and now she had to start over. She had to find a new job and become independent again. Out of everything that was going on, getting fired from her career wasn't sitting well with her. She was no longer letting Jordin ruin her life. She had go get away.

Jordin walked closer to the table and sat down at the other end of it. He pierced his eyes on Doll. His blood was hot, and he wasn't taking the situation lightly.

"So you really want out this marriage, huh? You want to leave me for some rich nigga you met in the club? You don't even know this nigga, and you're running off with him. I saw all your texts with him in your phone. I should kill him, and you if he comes here trying to save you. But I'ma let you out because I love you." Jordin grabbed the paper and pen and signed his divorce papers. After scratching his name on the paper, he slid it to her.

"Me wanting to leave you has nothing to do with me being with someone else. It's about you betraying me and leading me on. You could have left me alone if you knew marriage was too much for you, but you had to have me. You should have just stayed with Tiffany and ran the streets with her." She stood up. "I have to go."

She stuffed the papers in her purse and grabbed her rollaway luggage. Her heart was beating fast when she proceeded to walk past Jordin. She could feel him burning a hole in her flesh with his eyes. She knew he was angry, and she had a feeling he wasn't going to let her leave, so she picked up her pace. Right when she passed him, Jordin stood up swiftly and put a gun to her head. Doll froze and dropped her bag. Jordin turned her around and stuffed his gun in her face.

"Doesn't feel good to have a fuckin' gun pointed at you, huh, you stupid ass bitch? You think you can just leave me? After everything I've done for you?" Jordin snarled at her with a malicious look on his face.

Tears fell from Doll's eyes as he shoved the gun in her left cheek. She couldn't say a word, because she was so frightened. All she could think was he was going to kill her if she said the wrong thing.

"You said you'd rather die than be with me ... Well, I should kill you right now. You know how many people would miss your pretty ass if I killed you? You know your old ass daddy would have a heart attack if I took his precious baby girl out this world, so if I were you, I'd do what I say. Now get naked and go to the living room.

"Jordin, please. You don't have to do this. If you want to work things out, we can. Just don't kill me," Doll cried out, hoping he would change his mind. But the pill Jordin had taken before he came downstairs had kicked in full effect and was fucking with his emotions. Therefore, he wasn't sparing Doll anything.

"Bitch, you're only saying that because your life is on the line. After I kill you, I'm taking myself out. If I can't have you in life, then I'll follow you in death. Now take off your fucking clothes. I want to fuck you before we die."

Jordin walked her to the living room. He sat on the couch and pulled out his throbbing dick. "Get on your fucking knees and suck my shit."

When Doll got on her knees, Jordin put his gun to her head. "If you don't suck my dick right, I'm going to kill you before I even get to bust. And stop all that crying. That shit's making my dick soft."

Doll closed her eyes and put her mouth on his dick. Then she started sucking his dick like a pro, hoping he didn't kill her ...

$$$$$

Donni and Stacey pulled up to the address Doll had given him, at five on the dot. The sun was rising, and the temperature outside was cold. It had to be at least thirty-eight degrees. He looked in the driveway and saw a black Mercedes truck. He could see the lights shining in the home, so he knew somebody was there. The two got out his car and walked up to the door.

"You think we should knock or sneak in through a patio door?" Donni asked Stacey.

Stacey put his ear to the door. He didn't hear a thing. "Let's sneak around to the back and see if they have a sliding door. You know I can get in them muthafuckas with my knife."

The two snuck around the back of the house, and sure enough, there was a sliding door. But to their surprise, it was already unlocked. Donni slid the door open and pulled his pistol from his side. They started creeping through the dark den. They walked through the kitchen and made it to the dining room. When he made it to the living room, his temper flared quickly. Jordin was sitting on the couch with Doll in between his legs. He had his chrome gun to her head while she pleasured him with her mouth.

"That's right, lil' bitch. Top me off like a wife is supposed to do," Jordin said as he looked down at her.

Doll's face was full of tears. Jordin was treating her like an animal. Donni rushed behind Jordin and wrapped his arm around his throat and put his gun up to Jordin's head. Doll fell back when Donni lifted Jordin up from the couch by his throat. She was embarrassed and didn't know how much Donni had seen. Doll ran off up the bathroom while Donni and Stacey handled Jordin. She was so glad he had come in because she knew Jordin was going to kill them.

"So that's how you treat the woman you married, pussy? You force your dick down her throat, you sick ass nigga!" Donni shouted as he body slammed Jordin to the ground, almost breaking his back.

"Fuck you, nigga. You can have that broke bitch! The bitch was broke when I met her, and she's still broke! I was helping her out in this marriage. She ain't do shit for me!" Jordin shouted. Donni shoved his gun into Jordin's mouth, breaking a few of his teeth while forcing it in there.

"I should have killed your bitch ass when I had the chance. Yeah, nigga, remember when you were laid up in the hospital, shitting in a bag? That was because of me, nigga. I tried to take your bitch ass out. You played your homie Janario for some bread, and he wanted you dead. Now, I'm about to make that happen." Donni took his gun from his mouth and shoved it in his forehead.

"Fuck you, and fuck that nigga Janario! He'll never get his bread. That's my business; he doesn't own shit!"

"Whatever, nigga." Donni cocked his gun back, ready to blow out Jordin's brains. He hated niggas like Jordin and felt like he needed to take him out for every person Jordin had done wrong. He knew a lot of people would be happy when they got the news Jordin was dead. Stacey had put him up on game about Jordin when they were up drinking, and he found out Jordin owed a lot of people and had killed a lot of innocent people to get to the top of the drug game.

Before Donni could get his hands dirty, Stacey let off his desert eagle straight into Jordin's head. Donni backed away so blood wouldn't get on him.

"Thanks, bro," Donni said as he stood to his feet.

"You know I wasn't going to let you go out like that. You got a rep, my nigga. Now let's get ol' girl and get out of here. She ran off."

Donni walked around the house, looking for Doll. That was when he found one of the upstairs bathrooms and put his ear to the door. He could hear Doll crying and tossing things around.

"Dollaysia, it's me, babe. Open the door," Donni said as he knocked on the door.

Doll opened the door with a face full of tears. Donni walked in and took her into his arms.

"I'm so embarrassed! How could he do me like that?" Doll cried out in his arms.

"He's a sick mothafucka, and you won't have to worry about him anymore. He was wrong to treat you that way. But you are safe now. You're with me," he said as he walked her out the bathroom.

"Thank you so much for coming like I asked. He was going to kill me and himself."

"I know … My cousin popped that nigga, though, so let's get out of here. We can talk about it at my crib because you're going home with me."

"He's dead?" Doll asked in a sad tone.

"Yeah, that nigga's gone …"

Doll walked passed Jordin with her face buried in Donni's chest. She couldn't stand to see him dead. She didn't want the scene haunting her, so she walked out of the house, not seeing his body. Stacey grabbed her luggage and her purse and walked out with Doll and Donni.

Donni sat in the back seat while Stacey drove them to his house. The car was silent. All you could hear was Doll weeping in Donni's lap. When they arrived at Stacey's house, he and Stacey talked for a minute outside his car.

"You think she's going to be aight, man?" Stacey asked with concern in his tone. He had a wife, and he didn't know what he would do if that had happened to her. Stacey was hardcore. But he respected and cared for women. He would never degrade his wife or make her do things she didn't want to do.

"I think so. She didn't look at the body. But she's a little embarrassed about what we walked in on."

Stacey shook his head. "That shit is fucked up, bro. But let me get in here and explain everything to my wife. She's back with the kids."

"Alright, tell the misses I said hi."

They gave each other daps, and Donni walked to his driver's side. When he looked in the back seat, Doll was sleeping. He didn't want to wake her, so he hit the freeway and headed to his house he had in Westwood. When he got to his house forty-five minutes later, he parked in his six-car garage and carried Doll inside and to his bedroom. He placed her in bed and pulled his black sheets over her. He wasn't letting her out of his sight until he was comfortable with the situation, even though he knew there were some things she was going to have to handle since she was his wife. He hated that she had to deal with such a loser like Jordin, but he was going to be there for her every step of the way.

Donni went to his kitchen and made a few phone calls. He knew no one would be looking for Jordin until it was time for him to deal with his divorce, so he wanted to make sure the police didn't think Doll had anything to do with the murder. Therefore, he called a few people he knew to clean up the scene, and get rid of anything that Doll had left behind and Jordin's body.

$$\$\$\$\$\$$

Doll woke up five hours later in a huge king-sized bed. This time, she knew exactly where she was, and she felt safe. She sat up in bed and saw Donni sitting at the small desk area he had in his room. He was sitting on his laptop in a pair of basketball shorts, and he was shirtless. He was wearing a few gold chains around his neck and a pair of reading glasses on his face, making him look like a school boy.

"Is it still morning? I have to go mail these divorce papers. I know he is dead, but I still no longer want to carry his last name," Doll said as she ran her fingers through her mangled hair.

"Yes, it's still morning. I can have a driver take you where you want today. But are you sure you're ready to get out? You've been through a lot," Donni said, remembering everything that had happened earlier that morning.

"I know, but I got fired from my job, so I have to call my supervisor, and I know my mom is worried sick about me. I need to check on my apartment as well. It's just so much I have to do." She stood from bed.

"All that stuff can wait. Charge your phone and call your mom. Just stay here for the day, and you can handle everything tomorrow." Donni took his glasses off and stood up.

"I guess I can do that. I guess it all can wait." She sat down on the edge of the bed.

"You need food, and you need rest. I sent some of my peoples back to the house to clean up the mess and clean out all your belongings. I don't want the police looking for you for murder. If anything, they will contact you on a missing person because you were married to him. But I want to talk to you about a few things." Donni sat next to her.

"I really don't want to talk about what happened this morning. I'm too ashamed of what you saw me doing. And what do you mean, you got rid of the body? What kind of shit are you in where you can just get someone to remove a body and evidence." She stood up and crossed her arms. The last thing she wanted was another nigga doing dirt.

"I told you that I would be honest with you about everything, and I want to be honest with you about my past. I have connects when it comes to cleaning up a scene because I used to be a contract killer for a living. I wanted to tell you before somebody else told you and you think I was dishonest. I used to take niggas out for money, and Jordin was one of the last two niggas I was supposed to take out. But that's not why I came to save you. I had forgotten all about his best friend Janario hiring me and my cousin to kill him. He didn't die, because I had gotten sloppy and wanted out the business to open my gym. But me finding out he was the snake nigga that we didn't kill added fuel to the fire."

Doll looked at Donni and shook her head. He was telling her stuff that she couldn't even imagine him doing. He was successful, and he was a smart man.

Why did he have to kill people for a living in his past.?

So many questions crossed her mind, but most importantly, she was happy he was being honest.

"I always wondered who shot him that night. He was always so loved. I thought Janario was his boy." She sat next to Donni.

"Homies ain't loyal, and that nigga portrayed like he was loved, so many people feared him. That's why Janario hired us. Back then, Jordin owed Janario $90K, and there's no telling how much he owes him today. But he's going to be happy when my cousin delivers the news to him."

"I'm not mad at you about your past, and you don't have to tell me anything else about it if you don't want to. You have been real with me from the start, so I can't fault you for your past. Jordin was a bad person and deserved to be taken out. You're a good man, Donavan." She turned his face to hers so they could lock eyes. As much as she didn't want to fall for him so fast, he gave her a reason to.

"I just want to love you, Doll, and be there for you. That's why I'm telling you everything—so you can trust me."

"And I'm going to let you do that. I'd be a fool if I didn't." She kissed his lips.

Donni was taking her words as a yes. He was happy he was

changing her mind and opening up to him.

"You just made a nigga real happy, lil' mama. But you get some rest, and I'll wake you up to something nice. I'm not letting you out my sight, so prepare to be with me for a few days."

Doll sighed. "Okay, Donavan."

Doll stood to charge her phone so she could call her mother. Once her phone powered up, she immediately called her mom and assured her that she was okay. She told her mother that she was in Paris again and would be home in a couple days. She didn't want to tell her mother the truth and let her become worried and possibly tell her father. Her issue with Jordin was over, so there was no reason for her to worry. After she got off the phone with her mother, she showered in Donni's huge master bathroom. She enjoyed his waterfall showerhead for thirty minutes. She knew she was going to love living in luxury with Donni. He was classy, and he had a little bit of hood in him. She liked that, but she was happy he had changed his life around for the better, and that look looked even better on him. Doll stepped out of the shower. She didn't have anything to wear, and she had thrown her soiled clothes in the trash. She walked out of his bathroom in one of his fluffy black towels.

"If you need something to sleep in, you can look in my top drawer for a tank top," Donni said, pointing at his dresser.

"Thank you." Doll walked over to his dresser and pulled out one of his black tank tops.

She slid out of her towel, and Donni discreetly watched her every move as he pretended to turn back on his laptop. He watched how she slid the shirt over her head and how she pulled her natural hair into a pony. He thought she was so sexy and wanted to take her down. But he knew what she had just went through, so he decided to wait. He then watched Doll climb into his bed and pull the covers over her. She then watched him work until her eyes couldn't stay open any longer.

$$$$$

After working from his room for seven hours straight on his laptop, he realized it was five in the evening, and the sun was going down. He decided to shut down his laptop for the night and order Doll and himself some Italian food for dinner. He figured with everything going on, they could forget about carbs and pack them on for the night with a bottle of French wine. Doll had been working so hard to keep her life on track, so she deserved it.

He then climbed into bed while he waited for their food to be delivered. He began to spoon under Doll. She felt his body against hers and moved closer to him. He put his face in her neck and took in the smell of her bare flesh. Holding her felt so right. He started to feel his dick rise through his shorts, and so did Doll. She started grinding her ass on his pelvis. Doll started tugging at his basketball shorts, forcing them down. Donni slipped out of his shorts and pulled up the tank top she was wearing. No words were spoken as Donni kissed her neck and slid in and out of her. Doll let out a light moan as he slid inside of her slowly. Being woken up by him sliding inside of her felt great. Donnie pulled one of her breasts out her tank top and started playing with her nipples while he stroked her and sucked on her neck.

"You can cum inside of me again, baby. This time, I might be ovulating, though." She smiled in the dark, knowing he would be shocked.

"I thought you were on birth control?" Donnie asked as he continued to stroke her.

"I got off, so if you're ready to officially be with me, you'd do it."

Donni gave it no thought. He wanted Doll in his life forever. She was telling him things he wanted to hear, so he was going to put a baby inside of her like she wanted.

"If you want me to put a baby in you, I'ma do it." Donni pulled her closer and picked up his speed.

Doll placed her arm around the back of his neck as they tied their tongues together. From the way she was biting and sucking on his lips, he was ready to cum. After a few more strokes, Donni was coming inside of Doll like she wanted. They lay there kissing in the dark, not wanting to let each other go. Donni was so attached to her, and he loved the way she made him feel. He was hoping she was pregnant because he wanted to make his next move and make her his wife.

Donni's phone started ringing as his doorbell rang. He looked at his doorbell cam on his phone and saw that it was the food they ordered. He got out of bed and turned on the light.

"I got us some food. We're going to chill out and drink some wine over Italian food."

Doll smiled. "You sure know how to make me feel better."

"Always ..." Donni walked out of the room and got their food. They spent all night in his room eating, drinking, making love, and getting to know each other like no other ...

CHAPTER SIXTEEN

Five months later …

$\mathcal{D}$onni lay in bed with Doll with his arms wrapped around her, caressing her small round stomach. She was five months pregnant, and he couldn't be any happier. He had hit the jackpot the first time they tried, and now they were expecting a boy. Not only was Doll having his baby in a few months, Lisha was due to have his child at any moment. Lisha was keeping the sex a secret from him and told him that he would find out when she had the baby. He and Lisha were still rocky, but she did not interfere with him and Doll like she'd promised. He had been keeping tabs on Lisha to keep her calm, but she always found a way to argue with him. But he never let it get to him. They were in talks of giving him joint custody because Donni wanted to be in his child's life all the time.

As he lay watching TV over Doll's shoulder while she was sleeping, his phone started vibrating on the nightstand. He looked at Doll, and then he reached over to answer it. When he looked at his caller ID, it was Lisha. He answered, but before he could say hello, Lisha's mother was shouting through the phone.

"Donavan, you need to get to the hospital fast! Lisha is in labor! She has her boyfriend here, but she needs you!"

Donni sat up in bed and looked at the time. It was eleven at night. He didn't want to wake Doll, but he knew he had to be there to see his child born.

"Aight, I'm on my way." Donni hung up the phone and proceeded to wake up Doll.

"Babe, wake up. Lisha is about to have the baby, so I have to go to the hospital," Donni said as he shook her arm.

"Lisha is having what?" Doll asked in a sleepy and agitated tone. She hadn't heard about Lisha and her baby in so long that she had forgotten about them. He had kept his promise to her about keeping his drama away from her, and he had done just that.

"The baby. Remember, she is pregnant with my baby too?" he asked as he stood from the bed.

"Oh, yeah... *her*. Well, call me when the baby is born. Congratulations." She threw up the peace sign and threw the covers over her head. She didn't care about Lisha having her baby. She was tired and having her own baby in a couple months. She knew Donni wasn't with her or cheating with her, so she felt like there was no need for her to go the hospital with him. She wasn't his wife, and that was his responsibility.

Donnie walked into his closet and slipped on his black sweats and a hoodie. He slid on his Nikes and left the house. As he did eighty-five on the freeway in his black Tesla, his mind went into deep thought. He was about to be a father, and he knew that was going to change his life. He knew he wasn't going to be able to club like he used to or drink like he used to, and now he would be traveling with his children. He was going to let them explore the world with him and raise them like a father should. He already had plans to buy a house in Paris and upgrade his home in Westwood. His life had finally come together after so many setbacks when he lived his life as an assassin.

Donni drove into the hospital's parking lot and parked his car. He rushed into the hospital and went to the front desk. The nurse showed him where the maternity ward was, and a nurse showed him to Lisha's private room.

"Agghhh, this shit hurts!" he heard Lisha shout at the top of her lungs.

Donni walked into the room and saw Lisha lying in the bed in a hospital gown. Her hair was braided into two braids, and she had an oxygen mask on her face. Her mother was patting her face with a cold towel. As he got closer to the bed, he saw that her face was pale, and she didn't look like she was doing too good. But before he could say anything to her or her mother, the guy sitting next to Lisha's mother stood up and approached Donni.

"Yo, what the fuck is this nigga doing here? I thought you was done with this nigga, Lisha?" the man said with much base in his tone.

"Aye, I don't know who the fuck you is, my nigga. But I just came to watch my child come in the world. You can miss me with that drama shit," Donni said back to the man. He wasn't in the mood and didn't have time for any of Lisha's male friends and their jealousy.

"You wasn't thinking about your child being born when she was on bedrest for three months and couldn't work. I've been taking care of her. You got all that money and can't take care of the mother of your child," the man said as if he knew Donni. However, he felt like he did.

For the past four months that he had been with her, Mike had been taking care of Lisha hand and foot, paying her bills and her rent while she was on bedrest with a mild placental abruption while Donni paid her medical bills. Donni thought that was enough until the child was born. She hadn't told him about her being on bedrest, so he didn't know. But he wasn't with Lisha anymore, so he felt like he did not need to take care of her.

Lisha took the oxygen mask off her face. "Mike, don't start that bullshit. I'm laying here about to have a baby, and I'm in pain. I don't want to hear you arguing with my baby's father!" Lisha shouted as she felt a contraction coming.

"Nah, fuck that. This nigga gotta go," Mike boldly said as he got closer to Donni.

Donni smirked. "I gotta go? Nigga, this is my kid, not yours. You can fuck on Lisha all you want, but you don't run shit when it comes to my seed."

"Aghhh!" Lisha shouted again, but this time, she felt a puddle in between her legs. That was when her mother saw blood seeping through the white sheets. She laid her head back and arched her back. The pain was unbearable, and she wasn't feeling well at all. She knew something was wrong, and she knew she was having more than labor pains.

"Mike, you need to leave! I'm going to get a nurse; she's in pain!"

Lisha's mother said loudly as she stood up and grabbed Mike by the arm. She dragged him out the room with her so she could find the doctor.

At that moment, monitors around Lisha started buzzing and beeping constantly. Donni walked over to her bed and saw that her eyes were rolling in the back of her head. She was going into shock from losing so much blood. Donni lifted her body and held her close.

"You're gonna be alright, Lisha. You and the baby. Y'all good. Where the fuck is the nurses? She's going into shock!" He didn't want to worry, but her condition was stressing him out. Lisha was not doing okay, and the doctors or nurses hadn't come in.

When nurses and her delivery doctor came in, Lisha didn't have a pulse. Donni laid her head on her pillow and stepped back in total shock. His baby was still inside of Lisha, and she was gone.

"She doesn't have a pulse. We're going to have to cut this baby out of her. What happened, sir?" The doctor asked.

"She was losing too much blood and went into shock, and y'all took too long! Get my baby out of her before my child dies!" Donni said loudly, losing his cool. Things were going all wrong. He and Lisha didn't get along, because of their petty problems, but he didn't want her to die. She had so much to live for, like living for the baby she was having.

They rushed Lisha to emergency surgery. Donni paced as he waited for the doctors to let him know that his son or daughter was born. He didn't know what was going to happen now that Lisha was gone. He knew if his child were alive, he would still take care of his baby without her. But it wrecked his brain knowing he could possibly be a single father.

"Donni, I know we are both upset, but I need to talk to you," Lisha's mother, Lisa, said when she walked up to Donni.

They walked over to the waiting area and sat down. "What's up, Miss Lisa? I'm sorry for your loss. I felt fucked up holding her while she was dying and couldn't do shit about it. I know me and Lish had our problems, but she is the mother of my child. She didn't deserve to die." He put his head down and shook his head.

"I know you two had your problems, but that girl loved you. I don't know why she couldn't stay faithful to you, but she always said she wanted to do right by you." Lisa grabbed his hand and cuffed it into hers.

"I used to want to be with her too, but she pushed me away. My heart is in another place now. But now that she is gone, I know it's going to fuck me up. We were together three years; she was a part of my dream," Donni confessed.

At one point, he did love Lisha the same way he loved Doll. He thought he and Lisha had something and would be together forever. She was with him when he made his first million dollars, and she helped him with anything he had going on with his business. She had closed deals for him and saved his ass when he forgot about important things. But when they fell in love, things started to change, and it wasn't for the good. Lisha started using him for his title in the industry and started cheating with their clients that came to the gym. She got sloppy, and sometimes, it cost him money when she slacked on business.

"Well, I know this is a bad time, but we have to plan for the future now with that baby. I'm too old to take care of a young baby, and I don't have money to do so. Even if I adopt, I don't want to take care of anymore children. I took care of mine, and I just lost one, so you're going to have to take your child home with you. I can watch her because she is my grandchild, but I can't take her full time."

Donni sat silently. He and Doll had been planning for their new child, and he hadn't set up anything for Lisha's child. They were going to be going through a custody battle and a child support case when the baby was born, so he hadn't planned anything, because he was waiting for things to be settle in court first. But he knew he couldn't let his child go into the system since Lisa made it clear she wasn't taking the child.

"I guess I have no choice ..."

At that moment, the doctor and a nurse came out. They walked over to Donni and Lisa. "We were able to save your baby girl, sir. She is doing just fine and in the nursery. She lost little to no oxygen. You can see her."

"Well, I have to see what's going on with her mother, so go see your daughter," Lisa said with a slight smile. Her only daughter was deceased, but she gained a grandchild, so she had something to smile about.

When Donni laid eyes on his daughter, he felt butterflies in his stomach. When he laid eyes on her chubby cheeks and pretty, brown eyes when she opened them, he felt a different kind of love—a love that he knew would never break his heart. She was his baby girl, and he was going to do whatever he had to do to keep her safe. Once he held her, he knew there was no way he was leaving the hospital without her. She was perfect, and she was his.

"Your mommy is in heaven, lil' mama. But you're going home with your daddy to live a good life. Whatever you want, you can have it. You're my princess, and I love you already, little lady. Your mommy wanted to name you Chanelle, but I'm going to name you Nailah. It means 'beautiful' in African." He kissed her tiny hand. She started to cry just a little, getting the nurse's attention that was near. She walked over with a bottle. "She's hungry, sir." She handed him a bottle, and he started feeding his daughter.

"So I was just informed that the baby is well enough to leave tomorrow morning. But if you're going to take her home since you said you're the father, we will need to see proof, or she will be placed in her grandmother's care until you show us DNA," the nurse said.

"We did a DNA test before she was born. I have the paperwork in my briefcase in my car."

"Okay. Well, baby girl needs her rest. I have paperwork for you, and there's a social worker here to speak with you as well. They just want to make sure your daughter is going to be in good hands."

"Okay, that's fine."

After talking to social workers and signing the baby's birth certificate after he showed his DNA papers, Donni found himself asleep in the waiting area until seven in the morning when he was awakened by a nurse letting him know they were ready to discharge the baby. Donni was given everything he needed, and he left the hospital with his daughter in the car seat and a diaper bag her mother had for her in her room. He called his new assistant and asked her to bring a list of things for his daughter to his house. Now he had to head home and tell Doll everything that happened.

EPILOGUE

$\mathcal{D}$onni stepped out his car with a pink car seat in his hand, carrying his daughter. He was still in shock that Lisha had passed away in his arms, and he was now caring for his newborn daughter. He didn't know how Doll would feel, and he hadn't called her. He had been dealing with so much with social workers and Lisha's family that he didn't want to stress Doll out either. She was carrying their son, and now he was going to ask her if she could help him with his daughter. He knew that was probably going to be asking for too much, but he needed her to be a mother figure to his daughter.

Donni sat the car seat down and opened his front door. He walked down his long foyer that led to his living room. He tossed his keys on the table that was in his foyer and sighed as he made his way to Doll. When he walked into the living room, he spotted her sleeping on the couch with their comforter from their bed. The morning news was playing on TV as the sun peeked through the curtains. He sat the car seat on the loveseat and walked over to Doll. He took the covers from over her face and kissed her forehead. Doll slightly opened her eyes.

"Goodness, Donavan. Where the hell have you been? I've been calling you and worried sick." Doll sat up on the couch. When she sat up, she spotted the pink Eddie Bauer car seat sitting on the couch.

"A lot happened, Doll. Lisha died while in labor from a hemorrhage. Now I have full custody of my daughter." He wiped his hand over his face.

"Wow, Donni. I'm so sorry to hear that happened. Are you going to be okay?" Doll scooted closer to him and put her arm around his waist.

"I don't know. Maybe this is my karma. Me and Lisha had problems, but I never wished death on her."

"Babe, don't think like that. You got a baby girl now; that's a blessing. I'm so sorry about Lisha, but you're going to have to focus on baby girl. I'm going to be here to help you take care of her, so you won't be alone. I love babies," she smiled.

"That's why I would do anything for you, Doll. Thank you." He kissed her.

"I got your back, babe. We're in this together." Doll stood up and walked over to the baby. She lifted the receiving blanket and laid eyes on the prettiest baby girl. She picked her up immediately and took her into her arms.

"She's so beautiful and so small. She will be just fine with me. What did you name her?" Doll cradled the baby and walked over to Donni. She sat down next to him.

"I named her Nailah Chanelle Bradley."

"That's a beautiful name."

"My family is complete now. I just wish you'd change your mind about going back to work. You really don't need to. You can start your business like we talked about if you want to continue to show me your independence," Donnie said as he gazed at his daughter and Doll.

"I love you, Donavan. If you want me to stay at home with the kids like you said, I will do it now. I know we're not married, but you've already proven your love for me, so I won't be going back to work. I'll be starting my business," she smiled. She and Donni had been talking about her staying at home. She had applied for a few positions and had interviews in line. But now she was cancelling them all. She was going to be a stay-at-home mother and work on from home on her own fitness business. She wanted to be a wife and a mother like her mother, and she did not care how anyone felt about it.

"I love you too, Doll. And I'm happy to have you."

Doll was happy to have him too and glad she had finally gotten the man she deserved. She wasn't letting anything interfere with their small family they were creating. She was Donni's, and Donni was hers *forever...*

THE END!

Dear, readers!

I hope you enjoyed this story! Make sure you leave a review. Follow me on my social medias for updates! I love feedback, so flood me with it! Thanks for the support!

CONTACT THE AUTHOR

Instagram: BrandBulliesRobin

Text ROBINS NOVELS to 77948 for new release alerts

Website: https://www.novelsbyauthorrobin.com/

Facebook: https://www.facebook.com/AuthorRobinC

Looking for a publishing home?

Royalty Publishing House, Where the Royals reside, is accepting submissions for writers in the urban fiction genre. If you're interested, submit the first 3-4 chapters with your synopsis to submissions@royaltypublishinghouse.com.

Check out our website for more information: www.royaltypublishinghouse.com.

Do You Like CELEBRITY GOSSIP?

Check Out QUEEN DYNASTY!
Visit Our Site: www.thequeendynasty.com

Get LiT!

Download the LiTeReader app today and enjoy exclusive content, free books, and more

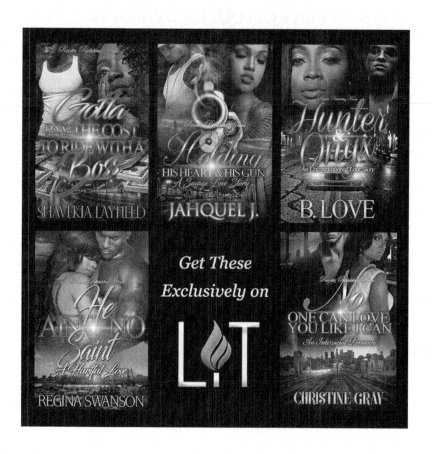

CPSIA information can be obtained
at www.ICGtesting.com
Printed in the USA
LVOW13s1916071117
555373LV00014B/1319/P